The Time Goblin

(book two)

By Simon Woods
Illustrated by Ralph Platt

Dedicated to my brilliant daughters, Molly
and Tilly. Enjoy

Special thanks go to Sophie Evans, William Irwin and Ben Tuffs for their general comments and general guidance.
I also have to thank, Yve, my wife, for her patience and ability to read and reread the ever developing story of Brave Dave and Tariq.
And finally a massive thank you to Mark Allen for proofreading a genre that is not part of his regular reading regime.

I am indebted to all of them.

Chapter 1.
Tariq's Soup and Door Knocking

Dave couldn't believe that anything untoward was going on. *Not in this world*, he told himself. NO—not in *his* new world; the unfeathered world, where people walked on the grass, and mud, and other stuff, and never wanted to flap their arms to leave the ground behind.

He grabbed the corner of the house and peeked out from the dark alleyway, as he looked towards the muddy and dingy garden once more. In its middle was a chicken wire and wood pen, the perimeter that enclosed his friend's hutch.

The tall man was still there, bent over the fence as he reached into Tariq's wooden box. Each time the man lent over the fence he thrust his hands into the hutch and pulled stuff from its insides. He turned as he push the contents into a black sack by his feet.

Dave shook his head. He couldn't believe Tariq had to live through this horror: If he did or could! Dave thought suddenly. The longer the man continued to thrust his hand into Tariq's hutch the more concerned Dave became.

After what seemed like the longest time that time could take—Dave hadn't properly adjusted to land-livers' time yet—the tall human shut the roof of Tariq's house, turned and tied the top of the sack up in a knot, then took the sack and put it in a tall green thing on wheels, next to the garden's shed.

Dave was worried. *What had the man done to Tariq's hutch? What had the man done to Tariq?* his mind asked. Dave really didn't know.

He watched closely as the lumbering man finished his tasks, and then walked towards a glowing light which shone from a place in the building's wall, a little distance from where Dave was hiding.

Dave waited. Nothing happened. And Dave watched. He was determined not to get caught. As nothing continued to happen Dave took a deep breath and stepped around the corner. His silhouette, his long dark shadow, stretched out behind him the further into the ominous light he stepped.

Nothing changed. After a moment Dave was sure he could make his way safely to Tariq's house. He needed to check if his new friend was okay, especially after the tall human's assault on his home.

Step by step Dave sneaked down the garden. Dave knew it would only be a few minutes before he'd be able to knock on his friend's door and find out how he was after the attack. If his friend was still there!

* * *

Tariq settled down for the evening. The Land Lord, for a change, had been a lot quicker cleaning his hutch this time.

Tariq just wished that the Tortoise Law, which prevented him from revealing his true nature, didn't exist. He didn't need a human to clean out his hutch, he was more than capable of doing it himself, and in fact he did, every day.

But when the Land Lord came, he had to muck up his beautiful home. Every time he had to make it look like, the version of a tortoise, one the Land Lord expected, was living right there in the hutch.

After many years of being the Jones' pet Tariq had finally designed the M.E.S.S system—an automatic system to litter his lounge with, what was essentially, mess; rank straw, rotting food matter, and something that looked like old tortoise poo.

The M.E.S.S system made his life as a pet a lot simpler, although he wished it wasn't necessary. But he was proud of his creation; the Muck, Effluent & Smelly Stuff system instantly filled the area of the hutch, an area the Land Lord expected to be filled, with everything the Land Lord believed should be there.

Tariq shook his head as he thought about it. The Land Lord didn't like clearing up the mess, and Tariq didn't like putting the mess there. But in this strange world both things had to happen to ensure Nature's harmony continued—the balance between people and the rest of life on the planet.

* * *

Tariq's kettle boiled, and the TV announced the programmes for the evening.

An evening of tea and TV, Tariq thought, he was happy. His life was getting back to normal after his strange meeting with the talking feather, a talking feather who wore a skin-tight yellow Lycra bodysuit, with a huge capital 'D' stencilled on its chest—a feather who liked to be called Dave. Tariq shook his head as he recalled the encounter. *A feather! In Lycra!* he sniggered to himself. *Who wanted to be called Dave!* Tariq chuckled. *How strange,* he thought, then, as his brows furrowed, *Who would ever want to be called Dave?*

As the kettle boiled his thoughts turned to the 'Tortoise Tall Story Talkathon'. An event which was going to take place in roughly five or six months' time. He couldn't wait to meet up with his friends and tell them about the strange day he'd had. He was sure they would wonder in disbelief as he told them about the amazingly weird feather from the sky; a feather who liked to be called Dave.

He was proud to go to the Talkathon and looking forward to it, especially as his mates had given him the title, 'Tariq The Gifted of the Insomniacs', although this version of his title wasn't quite the title he'd really been given. All that his tortoise friends had named him was 'Tariq of the Insomniacs', in recognition of his sleep problem. However, Tariq being Tariq, had ignored the fact, and added the words 'the gifted' to the title himself, and what a great title it was.

* * *

With the TV on, and the programme prior to his showing, he got up from the sofa and walked across the hutch to his kitchen: Tariq stood next to his white enamelled cooker and started the preparations for his evening meal. He was certain he'd be ready before 'The Great Tortoise Menu' started, although he hoped, this time, there'd be other culinary delights than the ones with lettuce—two whole series had been enough. But if he'd been invited then lettuce wouldn't be a problem as he'd be able to wow the judges with his speciality.

He closed his eyes as the idea of 'The Great Tortoise Menu' floated through his mind, with the contestants creating loads of different dishes, from all around the world, using carrots instead.

He pulled open a cupboard and took a lettuce from the shelf, then started to peel its leaves. One by one he dropped them into some boiling water; this was the beginning of his most excellent, 'hot 'n' soggy lettuce leaf soup'. And was just one of the culinary delights he was most expert at cooking. Or so he liked to think.

It was a dish that had never appeared on 'The Great Tortoise Menu' and because of this he knew he had to be one of the most excellent chefs of his time.

Tariq opened his fridge and removed three apples from its middle shelf, then dumped them into his smoothie maker. He whizzed up his preferred drink; there really was nothing better than 'hot 'n' soggy lettuce leaf soup' washed down with an apple smoothie.

He wondered whether he should write a lettuce soup cookbook and one day appear on the telly. "You never know," he muttered to himself, and smiled at the thought.

Whilst he waited for his soup to cook he sat back down on his sofa, then opened his local evening newspaper, the Daily Heron— as it had just been popped through his letter box.

To Tariq's surprise there was a photo, on page two, of someone he recognised, and although it was very blurry, and in black and white, he knew instantly it was a photo of the strange person he'd said goodbye to that morning. It was Dave, a strange sort if ever he'd met one.

The story went on to describe how a short and brown looking individual, wearing a bright yellow Lycra body suit, had caused havoc in a house just up the road and promptly disappeared without a trace!

Poor chap, Tariq thought to himself. *He's had it, he won't be able to go anywhere without being recognised now. If he's really lucky not everyone will believe what's written in the newspaper.*

Tariq's lettuce leaves were coming to the boil so he put down his newspaper and went over to the cooker to turn it off, then laid the table for dinner.

Tariq knew he was going to enjoy his meal *immensely*, especially as he was the lettuce soup expert.

Standing next to the cooker he decided to have a quick taste, and after a few spoonfuls, he spat it back into his saucepan, just like the experts would, or so he imagined. It needed a little more seasoning he'd decided. *Just tremendous*, Tariq nodded to himself, then crossed the kitchen to his pantry. He picked up the pepper and chilli ketchup from the shelf, then returned to his cooker and added the new ingredient to the soup.

Tariq decided to have a quick taste

After some vigorous stirring, he turned the cooker on again and waited for the soup to heat up. Once the soup started to boil he removed the saucepan from the cooker and poured himself a portion.

Sitting back at his kitchen table he took another sip of his delicious recipe, and for the second time he spat the soup out.

Ah yes!, Tariq thought. *I've forgotten the croutons*.

He returned to his kitchenette, opened the bread bin, took out a loaf of bread, cut a slice off and put it in the microwave for ten minutes.

Whilst the slice of bread was being turned into something that resembled a crouton, he spread out his food preparation cloth.

PING, went the microwave.

Tariq removed the slice of bread from the microwave and placed it at the centre of his crouton preparation cloth. Once done he folded the edges of the cloth over the microwaved slice.

CRUNCH.

Tariq slammed his crouton mallet down as hard as he could onto his cloth-covered microwaved bread; its hard and dried contents shattered.

Tariq picked up the cloth and emptied the contents into his palm. With the contents in hand he wandered back to the table and emptied the bread fragments into his bowl of 'hot 'n' soggy lettuce leaf soup'.

With a sigh of satisfaction he nodded; at last he could have his meal. Tariq supped a huge spoon's worth of his soup, then leapt back from the table dismayed.

"Errr... gazpacho! Tremendous!" There was one thing Tariq really didn't like, nor even wanted to get used to, and that was cold soup.

He picked up his bowl and poured the soup back into the saucepan, then put it on the cooker. He hoped this would be the last time he'd have to heat it up.

THUMP, THUMP, THUMP, went the door to his hutch.

"Don't even think it, Tariq," Shell shouted.

Shell was Tariq's imaginary friend. Someone he'd dreamed up, a person he could chat with over the lonely and cold winter months, whilst he waited for the spring to arrive, and along with it his tortoise friends.

He'd been doing this so long now Shell had become almost real, and she never failed to speak her mind. There was no getting away from her. She was Shell, his shell, and he had to live with the fact. But it was no comfort.

The door was thumped again

Chapter 2.
Lettuce Camouflage

Tariq steadied himself heeding Shell's warning. He dropped the spoon back into the saucepan of soup and looked toward his front door.

"Wh... who's there?" Tariq warbled.

"It's me—Dave," Dave shouted through the door.

"Dave? Is that you?"

"Yes! I just said it was—Is that you Tariq?" Dave asked, getting his own back for the ridiculous question.

"Yes...," Tariq replied. His brows furrowed as he attempted to work out what was going on.

"Tariq the Gifted of the Insomniacs?" Dave continued his questioning.

"Yes," Tariq said once again. It was now apparent that Dave knew who he was. But it was beyond Tariq as to why Dave was asking the strange questions.

"Thought so," Dave said.

Tariq made a decision against his better nature. "Hey," he said. "Dave, come on in."

He was surprised at the return of the strange feather. It hadn't been something he'd expected.

"Can't," Dave replied.

"Can't?" Tariq repeated. He was even more confused. And, once more, his brows were making an attempt to cover his eyes as they furrowed.

"Yep," Dave agreed, "I can't," he said again.

"Why not?"

"You need to open the door," Dave explained.

"Oh... that. Just slide the bolt."

"Can't," came Dave's simple answer.

"Why not?" Tariq asked, even more perplexed.

"You've put your sign back up."

"What sign?"

"The sign that says, *'For Tariq's use only. In case of emergencies'.*"

"Oh yeah!" Tariq said as he remembered. He made his way to the door of his hutch and opened it. "Dave!" he said. "Well, well, well," he finished.

"Yes," Dave responded. "Thanks, thanks, thanks," he said. "Are you?" Dave asked.

"What?" Tariq said as he frowned again. His brows were beginning to ache with all the exercise they were getting.

"Well?" Dave answered.

"Yes," Tariq said, still not sure what was happening.

"Well, well, well," Dave said.

"What?"

"Oh nothing. Good to see you again, Tariq."

"Actually, Dave, it *is* good to see you again too."

"You won't believe what happened to me today." Dave really needed to tell someone about his day. He hoped Tariq would listen.

"Won't I?" Tariq asked. But before Dave could respond Tariq continued, "Come on in, Dave. Have a seat, sit down." Dave entered

Tariq's hutch and sat down on his tatty brown leather sofa.

Dave stared silently at Tariq. Tariq looked back at Dave.

"Well?" Tariq asked.

"Thought you'd never ask," Dave said as he smiled, then began to tell the tortoise all about his adventure.

Enthralled, Tariq sat and listened to Dave's story only butting in once to ask him what he meant by the 'concrete causeway'. Dave described the long flat hard thing which lay between two grass strips in front of the house he'd gone to.

"Oh! You mean the road."

"Do I?" Dave asked, not ever having had any experience of roads before.

"Of course you do," Tariq said.

"All right then; the road." Dave continued his story. When he got to the bit about the apparition, its eyes and the pitchfork, Tariq started to quiver and shake. Dave's story was not making him feel happy at all, especially as night had fallen.

"Tremendous! You did all that?" Tariq questioned; anything to change the topic. "At least I know more about you," he concluded.

"What's that?" Dave asked, curious.

"You're the bravest feather I've ever known. Admittedly, the only feather I've ever known, but brave nonetheless."

"I wouldn't call it brave," Dave said. "It was something I just had to do."

BANG... KERCHINK... CHING, CHING, CHING.

Dave, you've turned green!

Tariq disappeared into his shell trying not to disturb her too much on the way.

"O," went Dave, cut off in mid-Oh. "Clop," Dave continued.

Silence descended.

A few moments went by then Tariq popped one of his eyes out of the top of his shell, for a quick look around.

"Aaaaaarrgghhhhh," Tariq screamed. "Dave..., Dave, what was that?..., Dave you've turned green. Daavveee," Tariq finished, popping his eye back into his shell.

"Blop," Dave replied, then continued in a low moan, "oooooooooohhhhhh," adding finally, "ow, ow, ow", when he'd managed to clear his mouth of green goo.

After a short pause Tariq popped his head out of his shell, and looked around his hutch.

His eyes were instantly drawn towards his front door where an almost flat circular silvery addition to its surface, could be seen sticking from it.

"FLYING SAUCERS!" squealed Tariq. "No," he added, quickly changing his mind with a huge sigh of relief. "Flying saucepan lid— Phew—Dave what happened to you?" Tariq asked as he noticed Dave had somehow turned completely green.

"Oh… Nothing really," Dave responded to Tariq's question. "I just decided to explode. Nothing much, the truth be told." Dave paused for a moment to see if the tortoise had 'got it', but nothing had registered with Tariq. So Dave continued. "Then, following my explosion, I decided to remove my lettuce-leaf camouflage suit which, fortunately, I had with me in a concealed pocket, so I could put it on for your pleasure; and I did all that whilst swallowing part of the suit for my final trick."

"Really?" Tariq asked. He was extremely impressed.

"NO! Not really you daft tortoise. Some idiot left a pan of boiling lettuce on the cooker." Dave licked his lips, "with added chilli, tomato and..." Dave licked a lump of old soggy crouton from the corner of his eye, stating finally, "and bread."

"Oh," Tariq answered, sheepishly. He'd forgotten about his most excellent culinary delight, the one which he was going to write cook books about.

Tariq looked at Dave just in time to see Dave attempt the delicate extraction of lettuce leaf bits from his right ear.

"Sorry," Tariq said.

"Don't look," Dave insisted.

"Why?"

"Just don't. Okay?"

"Okay," Tariq agreed and popped his head back into his shell.

Dave stood up and started the 'sacred wet dirt removal dance'. All the green goo slid from him into a puddle, on the floor. Dave stepped out of the puddle and sat back down on the sofa looking as fresh as the day he had been shed.

"Okay. You can look now," he said.

Tariq popped his head out of his shell, now he'd been allowed.

"How did you do that?" Tariq questioned; he was intrigued, and the fact he was an engineer only made him more in need of the answer.

"Don't think about it, Tariq. It's a secret; and that's all I can say," Dave said.

Chapter 3.
The Problem with Wind

"Go on, Dave, tell me the rest," Tariq prompted. "Except how you managed to get rid of all that goo, of course," he added. Although he desperately wanted to know how the feather had cleaned the goo from itself, so quickly; as far as Tariq was concerned, for the moment, Dave's secret would have to remain a secret. It wasn't as if Tariq didn't have his own little secrets as well.

Dave went on to tell Tariq how he'd managed to thwart the apparition's attempts to move the pencil case, and how a horrible rotting green hand had appeared from nowhere to zap the apparition into nothingness.

"So, that's what happened to me," Dave finished.

"Wow!" Tariq was truly amazed. This story would definitely go down well at the 'Tortoise Tall Story Talkathon'.

"There's one thing that still bothers me about the whole adventure though," Dave said.

"What's that?" Tariq asked.

"Why on earth do I keep being lifted, from the ground, thrown this way and that, by something I cannot see?"

"You're a feather," Tariq explained, "albeit not a typical one".

"Really? A feather?" Dave responded: As if he didn't know what he was.

"Yes really," Tariq nodded as he answered.

"I know that. But what's that got to do with the price of fish?"

"Nothing. But you're as light as air, or should be."

"And?" Dave said.

"It's wind."

"I beg your pardon?" Dave sniffed, nope nothing was going on there.

"No. Wind, air wind," Tariq said sensing Dave's embarrassment.

"Air wind?" Dave thought about this concept. "Okay, tell me more." He was not entirely sure what Tariq was going on about.

"Movements of air created by differences between areas of high pressure and areas of low pressure, in the atmosphere," Tariq said.

"Low pressure and high pressure?" Dave repeated as he attempted to get the idea straight in his head. "Let's see if I've got this right," Dave continued. "What you're saying is that differences in the thickness of the air, with the high pressure air being thicker air, and low pressure air being thinner air, causes the stuff the air is made from, to move from the thicker air in the direction of the thinner air, and it's these movements that make me move?"

Tariq sighed with relief. "Yes. Exactly!" he said.

"Doesn't fit with what happened to me. There wasn't any of this wind today."

"Ah! Now you're talking about induced pressure."

"Induced pressure?" Dave queried, confused about his problem again.

"Yeah; the pushing of air, say, by an apparition, from one place to another, making the air left behind, after the pushing, a lot thinner; a gap in the air, if you will. And the air where the other air has been pushed to, a lot thicker, because there is more of it in the same place."

"Right?" Dave said as he scratched his head, hoping it wasn't going to start hurting.

"It is the gap that has to be filled with the air, which is not as thin, which makes the movement. That is; the thicker air around the gap thins out to make itself as thick as the thin air, by making the thin air thicker until they are the same," Tariq explained. "Thickness," he added, quickly.

Dave gulped. He wasn't sure his newly found brain was able to cope with the things Tariq explained. Everything was sloshing around in his head. But he concentrated, and tried hard to understand. "So," Dave started, "when the air moves from where it is to where it isn't anymore, this creates the movement, and it is this movement which moves me around, as if I didn't have anything else better to do?" Dave half closed his eyes as he finished, and stared at his friend.

"Exactly," said Tariq and smiled. Perhaps the feather wasn't as daft as it seemed.

"Why?" Dave asked.

"Why?" Tariq repeated.

"Yes. Why?" Dave said again.

"Erm—," Tariq tried to think of a reason. Then it popped into his head. "Because you're a feather," he said.

"Yes—I know that. But what's that got to do with the price of fish?"

"Nothing. But you *are* as light as air." Tariq stopped and looked at Dave. He felt like the whole conversation was going to be utterly pointless.

Dave was smiling. "Sorry, Tariq. I do get it really."

"Good," Tariq responded, not impressed one bit.

"But how am I going to get around this problem? It's not very helpful when I'm trying to do good and great deeds, as it is my destiny to do—for I am the helper of all living things, and without my destiny I have nothing. Nobody to help, and no reason to be."

"Believe it or not, I've already thought about that, Dave."

"You have?" Dave said stunned.

"Yup."

"How?" Dave responded.

"A machine."

"A machine?" Dave questioned.

"Yes—a special machine. A very special machine indeed," Tariq continued. "One that will increase your weight so that air will treat you with the same respect as it treats concrete."

"And what way would that be?" Dave asked.

"Heavier," Tariq said quite seriously. "I, Tariq," he prattled on, "will build this machine for you. This machine will be unlike any other ever created before. A machine that will give you powers of the like never seen or felt on this plane. A machine that will be known as the '*Concretonator*'!"

"The Concretonator?" Dave repeated. "Aren't you getting a bit carried away?"

"No. There is one thing I know for sure, and that is this; concrete is heavier than air."

"Everyone knows that," Dave said.

"I know. But not everyone has that power, the power to make air treat you just like it treats concrete."

"And how, exactly, is that?" Dave asked.

"NOT. AT. ALL!!!" Tariq pronounced each word, slowly and individually, as he attempted to be very clear about what he meant.

Dave could almost hear the drum rolls. "Okay. Let's do it!"

The two new friends looked each other in the eye and nodded. The course of the next hours had been determined.

Chapter 4.
Into the Laboratory

"Follow me," Tariq said to Dave as he grabbed the feather's arm, and led him towards the back of his hutch.

From floor to ceiling the back wall was covered by a grimy rug. It was a rug you'd normally find covering someone's floor; it had tassels around its edges, and, for the most part, it was a very dark brown. But at its centre it had dark orange and dark green diamond patterns criss-crossing its middle.

Tariq grabbed the edge of the rug and pulled it to one side. But there was no wall behind it as one would expect; just a doorway that had been hidden.

"How is that going to help me?" Dave asked as he stared at the newly revealed door.

"It won't," said Tariq as he smiled. "But it is what's behind this door that will help you."

Dave stared at Tariq and wondered what could possibly be behind the door. Truly! Something that could help him? Then he wondered whether his new tortoise friend might just be, somewhat, mad.

Tariq pushed open the door, and a staircase down into the ground below Tariq's hutch, came into view.

"A staircase?" Dave observed. Dave was finding it difficult to work out how some steps would help him get over his wind problem.

"Not just any staircase, Dave," Tariq said. "But steps into a special place; a place where I create all my inventions."

"Oh!" Dave said, surprised. It hadn't occurred to him that Tariq could possibly create inventions, whatever they were. But being new to the world Dave was willing to accept anything and everything. Mostly!

Tariq reached into the passageway and flicked a switch. A single bulb on a thin wire hung from the ceiling above the stairs. It lit up the thin dingy wooden stairway.

"Come with me," Tariq said in a low and ominous tone.

The tortoise and feather descended the dim staircase. Dave followed Tariq. Every now and then Dave looked back up the stairs and wondered whether he was doing the right thing.

At the bottom Tariq flicked another switch and a huge box-like cavern came into view; the cave illuminated by rows of strip lighting;

many, many tubular lights exposed its vastness.

The weird laboratory had been carved out of the soil below Tariq's hutch. Dave was astounded. It must've taken Tariq years to make. But, to Dave, Tariq didn't look old enough.

Dave looked around the dank room. Stacked on the shelves, and on the floor, were all kinds of mechanical bits and pieces.

"What do you think?" Tariq asked.

"Well," Dave said, "it's a brown dank room with lots of bits of machinery and other stuff."

"Not quite," Tariq said. "This is my laboratory. This is where I do all my experiments during the winter; where I design my machines, and create exotic food dishes, such as my 'hot 'n' soggy lettuce soup'."

"Really?" Dave said and raised an eyebrow; he wasn't quite sold on the idea— yet.

"Yes," said Tariq with utmost sincerity. "And this is where we will build the Concretonator."

Dave was not certain about this proposal. *How can someone*, he thought, *a person who cannot boil lettuce successfully, be relied upon to devise, and then create, a machine like the Concretonator? Oh well*, he sighed to himself.

"Okay," Dave replied. "Where do we start?" Dave felt this was probably not the right thing to say. *But hey*, he thought, *let's give the guy a chance.*

Tariq wandered to the back of the lab, opened a drawer, and pulled out a huge piece of paper with all sorts of diagrams scrawled across it.

"When did you start designing this thing?" Dave asked. The revelation had made him curious. It was obvious to him there was no way Tariq could have known of his upcoming reappearance at his front door.

"A long time ago, Dave. But this design is not exactly the design of the Concretonator. It's just something I was working on in order to give Shell a chance for a holiday, without me. The machine was designed to give me an artificial shell while she was away, but I never got around to finishing it."

"Who's Shell?" Dave asked.

Tariq, not wanting to be thought of as slightly mad, ignored the question and carried on. "Well, as I see it, you need a *shell* of sorts; something you can wear to stop the problem you have with the wind—a shell suit." Tariq chuckled to himself and Dave looked at him blankly.

"I don't have a problem with wind, Tariq. Thank you very much. It's air wind," Dave stated for the record.

"Okay. I understand what you're saying, Dave," Tariq said. "Now, all I need to do is change the design so that when the machine's turned on it works to your size."

For the next couple of hours Tariq took Dave through the machine's design. He described all the parts they would need to build the Concretonator. Once Tariq had finished, they started the work.

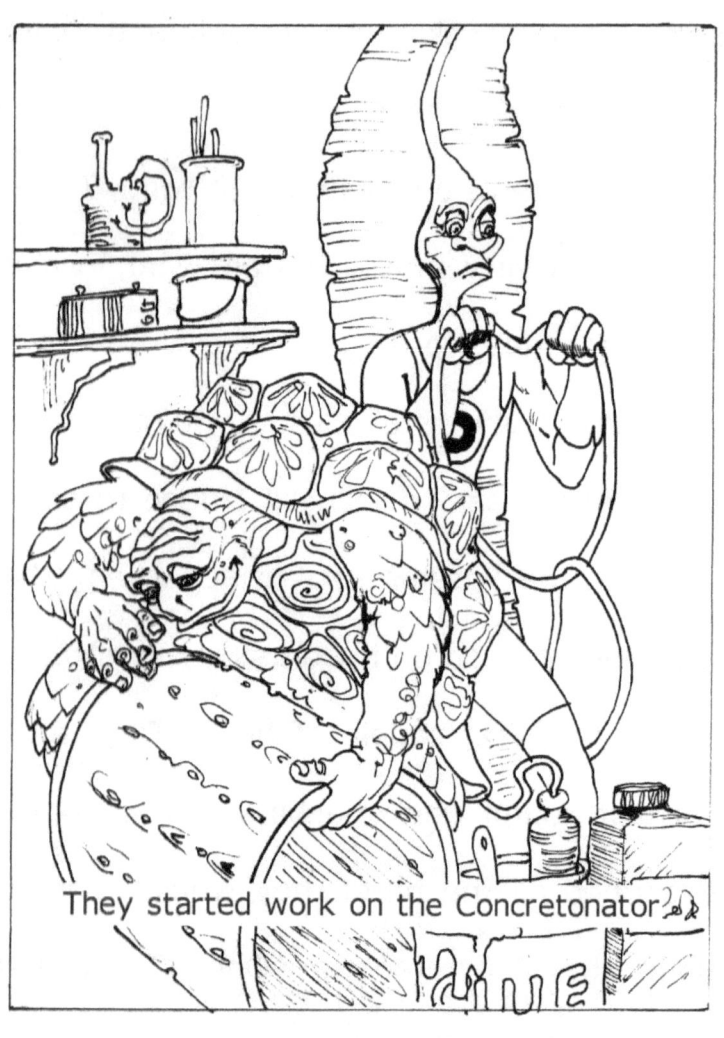

They started work on the Concretonator

Dave and Tariq rummaged through the lab

pulling the necessary bits and pieces from the shelves, dumping them all in the middle of the lab's floor.

A tumbler out of a tumble dryer, the inner tubes of bicycle tyres, motors from food mixers, big vats from ice cream vans, pots of glue, a bag of cement, some canisters of cod liver oil, a remote control from a DVD player, the insides of an old computer and, finally, a hose.

When they'd finished Tariq declared with some glee, "We're ready to start building the Concretonator."

"Have you ever built a machine from one of your designs before?" Dave asked.

"Yes—sort of—no—I suppose not," Tariq said. "I haven't really had the time, what with the creation of the most excellent culinary delight."

"And what was that?"

"Hot 'n' Soggy lettuce soup with chilli tomatoes," Tariq said.

"Surely it couldn't have taken that long," Dave observed.

"To get these things absolutely right does take some time you know."

"How long?" Dave said.

"About six years," replied Tariq.

"Six years!" Dave said stunned. "For a soup? A soup you still haven't got the hang of?"

"To get such things right takes time you know," Tariq repeated.

"Okay. So what you're saying is that you've never ever, ever, built a machine you have designed, ever before, because you were working on your soup?"

"Yep. That's about the long and short of it," Tariq concurred.

"And you don't see any problems, at all, with what we're trying to do now?" Dave asked.

"Nope. Why should I?"

"No reason, just wondered." Dave was becoming very worried about the whole project. However, he dismissed his worries; he knew that if he was to fulfil his destiny then something had to be done about his wind problem. Not being able to see any other way to make the situation right, Tariq's machine would have to do.

Dave decided to go with it. What's the worst that could happen? he wondered.

Tariq pulled an old stainless steel, food preparation table from the depths of his lab. "This will be the chassis," he declared as he patted the table's top.

They picked bits of machinery from the middle of Tariq's lab's floor as they got to work. First they manoeuvred the vat from the ice cream van and placed it on to the top of the steel table.

Tariq crossed the lab, opened his tool box and lifted out a huge drill. After he'd plugged it into the wall socket, Tariq drilled a few holes in the ice cream container, then sliced up the hose and bicycle inner tubes with a pair of garden shears, and attached them to the fledgling machine.

Working busily, Dave and Tariq continued to add the other bits and pieces from the lab floor to the table and ice cream container.

By four in the morning Tariq declared the machine finished. Dave looked at it astounded. It actually looked like a machine, with funnels, and switches, and tubes all joined together. Dave was rather impressed. But it hadn't been turned on yet.

Dave decided he would wait until the machine had been shown to work, in the way it had been designed, before helping Tariq any further.

"I'm tired, Tariq. What else is there to do?" Dave said.

"Not much. You go upstairs and get some sleep. I'll add the final touches," Tariq said;

still full of energy and with no sign of fatigue or tiredness.

Dave wandered back up the dingy wooden staircase into Tariq's hutch, and aimed straight for the very comfortable looking bed. He was asleep almost before his head hit the pillow.

Chapter 5.
Nightmares

Dave was dreaming about the days before he'd been given the life of an individual: The life before he'd been set free.

He was back with his crowd of other feathers. They were working together, in unison, as they flew over Dover and then the English Channel. And he was happy. Not a care in the world—that was the job of their host, Jonesy the buzzard, who thought he was a swan.

Dave listened to Jonesy honk, or as near to honking as the buzzard could manage. He heard the other swans reply as their wedge, the group they were a part of, soared through the sky above the twenty-one mile expanse of sea between England and France.

The weather changed quickly; the blue skies replaced by angry clouds. Vicious grey roiling cotton wool globs repealed the sky's nicety.

Soon the wedge started honking more and more. The calls were worried and frantic, and the sky darkened and the wind picked up.

The flight to France got worse and unpleasant. The air became bumpy as the wind increased, and along with it the turbulence, which made the air feel like a rough road full of ruts and humps and lumps. So much so that all the feathers, Dave's brothers and sisters, were finding it very difficult to keep Jonesy, his father, his creator of sorts, *their* father, in the air and above the sea.

Then, all of a sudden, they were headed straight down, beak first, towards the dark foam-crested waves of the miserable grey sea below. There was no land in sight, no land where they could shelter. The sky blackened further.

Jonesy didn't seem to be bothered at all by the situation. But Dave, or Seventh of Nine Thousand, Three Hundred and Forty Two (feathers), as he used to be known, sometimes Seventh for short, knew they were in terrible trouble. He couldn't understand why no one seemed concerned. Why Jonesy wasn't making any effort to pull up and make land. Why none of his feather brethren were trying to stop the descent.

Jonesy could not float, nor could he swim, because poor old deluded Jonesy was a buzzard, and not a swan as he thought he was. And he was definitely not aquatic as the orphaned Jonesy had assumed from a very early age, though he'd never, ever, dipped so much as a claw into a river or a stream.

Jonesy hit the water, hard. After some surprise at the new knowledge he didn't have any idea about swimming, or how to stay afloat on water successfully, for that matter, poor old Jonesy started to sink as his feathers became waterlogged.

Seventh and his colleagues were dragged under the sea, not able to breathe, and not able to take to the air again. Water rushed around them, soaked them, made them heavy. Jonesy's feathers were not made the same way the feathers of water birds were; his didn't repel the water so easily.

Seventh blinked and tried to understand what was going on around him. He tried to control the panicked thoughts which threatened to take over his mind.

"Hoob berberler." He heard as he went under the surface. "Ber ber her ber ler hayve," the noise continued as Seventh sank deeper, and deeper, and deeper beneath the waves.

"Hayve hake hup ber ber ler," the strange voice went on.

Dave blinked. *Turtles?* he thought. *Oh no! I'm truly sinking.*

"Dave, wake up," Tariq said again, he was very worried. He tried to shake Dave awake.

"I THINK YOU MIGHT BE HAVING A DREAM, DAVE! CAN YOU HEAR ME?" Tariq had grabbed Dave by the shoulder straps of his running suit, and lifted the unconscious feather so they were almost nose to nose.

Tariq decided he was probably better off with the problem of not being able to sleep, especially if the dreams Dave had had, had made him feel so bad, so worried; scared even.

Dave's eyes opened slowly. After a few moments Tariq's concerned face came into view. Dave sighed with relief, but the relief was only temporary.

"Dave, it's the morning," Tariq beamed at his guest. "The machine, the Concretonator, is ready for you," Tariq continued. "And it's time to test it," he added. He was very excited.

Dave shuddered. The thought of what could happen next with the Concretonator was even more horrible to think about—much more so than the dream he'd just been roused from.

Tariq looked at his new friend and saw the way he was. "Perhaps some refreshments first?"

Dave nodded.

"Tremendous," Tariq said.

Chapter 6.
Olive Oil and Cement

After a cup of tea Dave began to feel a bit more like his new self. He followed Tariq back down into the lab.

"What's in there?" Dave said as he pointed at a huge container of grey, oily looking slurry, which was sitting on top of the stainless steel table.

"That's what your shell will be made of," Tariq said.

"Yes. But, what's in there?" Dave continued his questioning.

"Well, it is a delicately balanced emulsion, a mixture of very, very, very small lumps in liquid. Sort of like paint but not, solely designed to give you a comfortable freedom of movement. The shell will form around you when the emulsion has been ejected from the Concretonator."

"Tariq, just tell me what's in there," Dave said. He was concerned about what was probably going to happen next.

"Olive oil and—cement," Tariq replied, giving up on the idea of keeping the ingredients of Dave's shell suit from him.

"OLIVE OIL? AND CEMENT?" Dave repeated, exasperated.

"Don't worry, Dave," Tariq said. "It's been specially formulated," he finished. He hoped his last statement would make Dave feel calm and more comfortable with the answer. But his hopes were unfounded.

"You've got to be kidding!" Dave blurted.

"Honestly, Dave, it's okay. Trust me, I'm a tortoise."

"AND?" Dave said, not feeling any reason whatsoever to accept Tariq's explanation, even if he was a tortoise.

"Dave, it is far better to trust and be disappointed in a tortoise, than to distrust and be disappointed in strife," Tariq responded as he attempted to sound wise in his answer to Dave's question.

"What's that supposed to mean?" Dave said.

"I don't know, but it's probably relevant."

After a few moments thought Dave sighed a huge sigh. "Okay, Tariq, what do I need to do now?"

"Tremendous! Right!" Tariq grinned. He was relieved he wasn't going to be pushed for any further answers. "Go over there," Tariq said pointing, "and stand in that specially constructed cabinet."

Dave looked in the direction his friend had indicated. "You mean that old shower cubicle?"

"Yes. But it's a specially constructed old shower cubicle," Tariq confirmed.

Dave wandered over to the cubicle and stepped into it, then asked, "What do I do now?"

"Nothing. Just put on those eye protectors," Tariq said as he pointed at the goggles which hung from a peg on the wall of the cabinet, "and hold your arms out horizontally."

Tariq picked up the Concretonator's plug and pushed it into a free power socket on the wall, then pressed the on switch.

The food mixers' motors, which were now part of the Concretonator, whirred into life and the 'specially formulated' olive oil and cement slurry started to circulate around the ice cream vat.

Tariq strolled back to his machine and unclipped the hose from its side, and pointed its nozzle at Dave.

What am I doing? Dave thought to himself.

"Ready, Dave?" Tariq asked.

"I suppose so," Dave said reluctantly.

"Arms out then," Tariq commanded, then started his count down. "Five, four, three, two, one, Concretonator away!" Tariq twisted the valve, which he'd attached to the end of the hose on his Concretonator machine, and from it shot a jet of lumpy, yellowy grey mixture.

Five, four, three, two, one, Concretonator away!

Dave felt the impact from the jet of slurry

directly on his chest as the mixture started to cover him.

Tariq turned up the pressure and the force on Dave's chest increased. To Dave's shock and dismay the increased force sent him smashing through the back of the cabinet, only to be halted by the wall behind it.

To Dave's dismay the force sent him crashing through the cabinet.

Dave was now some five metres away from

the cabinet, and stuck to the wall, one metre above the floor of Tariq's lab.

"SSTTOOPPPPPPP," screamed Dave.

"What's that, Dave? I CAN'T HEAR YOU," Tariq shouted, as he attempted to be heard over the noise of the Concretonator.

"BLOBBBB, BLOP, BLOBBBB," Dave said, his mouth completely covered by the Concretonator's thick sludge.

"SORRY, DAVE," Tariq shouted again. "I still can't hear you. I'm going to have to turn the machine off. Is that okay?"

"YOB," was the only answer Dave was able to give.

Tariq closed the hose's valve, wandered back to the wall socket and turned the power off. The noise from the Concretonator died away.

Tariq looked at his cabinet. "Oh!" he said, as he noticed Dave was no longer there, and somehow a huge hole had appeared in the back of it.

Tariq walked up to the cabinet, stepped in, and looked at the hole. He poked his head through and looked at the wall behind.

Tariq frowned, somehow the wall of his lab had been changed. He looked harder, then spotted it. In the middle of his lab's back wall he noticed a large yellowy dark-grey blob, which lightened as it dried.

"Ah!" he said as he realised what had happened—and where his friend was now located. "You okay, Dave?" he whispered, not really wanting a response, something that would indicate his friend was injured, or worse—injured to death!

As Tariq watched the yellowy light grey lump peel slowly from the wall he prayed to the tortoise deities for Dave's health.

Top first the dried blob came away from the wall. Then, with gravity in control, it crashed to the floor and shattered into hundreds of pieces.

Dave lifted himself from the shattered grey blob. As he stood he shook his left arm in an attempt to rid it of a particularly stubborn lump of concrete mixture, a lump which had stuck fast.

"What are you trying to do to me, Tariq? Kill me?" Dave said, still trying to shake the lump of slurry from his arm. "Look at this, Tariq," he continued, and lifted his left arm and waved it in Tariq's direction.

"I think I need to reduce the power in the motors," Tariq said. "What do you think, Dave?"

"What do *I* think?—I think you're mad. That's what I think," Dave said in a huff.

"Come on, Dave, calm down. It was only the first test. You can't expect things to go perfectly first time. Please be reasonable."

"Calm down? Reasonable? First test?"

"Yes. I mean, you're not a giver-upper are you?" Tariq accused.

Unfortunately for Dave there was only one answer he could give to this question, even after everything he'd been through.

"No," Dave sighed, beaten. "I'm not." And he wasn't.

"Right. All I have to do now is reduce the power and modify the emulsion slightly. Then we'll be ready to go again once I've repaired the cabinet. Why don't you put the kettle on?"

"Okay," Dave said. He was beginning to understand why he'd been so concerned in the first place. Dave left the lab and made his way up the stairs to Tariq's kitchenette, then put the kettle on.

Dave knew he had to carry on with this experiment as there was really no other way, that he could see, to get over his wind problem.

Tariq retrieved the Concretonator design from the drawer and examined its details once again. He was certain he'd missed something, but was not quite sure what it was. An hour later Tariq understood the error.

Ah! The current mixture is not flexible enough, he thought to himself. *What I need is something to make it more rubbery.*

Tariq looked around his lab and all he could see were some spare car tyres.

Right! Tariq thought, then ran up the stairs to his kitchen.

"Hi, Dave," Tariq said as he entered his lounge.

"Oh!—Hi," Dave said

"Not ready yet, but I will be soon," Tariq enthused.

"That's really fantastic, Tariq. Really?" Dave asked.

"Yeah," Tariq said. "Don't you think this is tremendous?"

Oh great, Dave sighed inwardly, not bothering to answer.

Tariq opened the kitchen cupboard and pulled out a food blender, and a bottle of stain remover, then shut the cupboard door, opened another and removed a box of unused mothballs, then rushed them all back down to his lab.

Dave didn't have a clue what was going on. He was only certain that this would mean more testing, and that he would have to be a part of it.

* * *

Tariq plugged the food blender into the nearest socket as he lifted off its lid. He then cut bits from the car tyres and put them into the blender. Once it was half full he replaced the lid and turned the blender on.

The food blender began to judder, but as the tyre clippings were gradually shredded into smaller pieces it steadied itself.

When the blender was steady Tariq added the mothballs, and after the usual juddering the food blender contained a powdered mixture of car tyre and mothballs.

Tariq continued with his plan and poured the stain remover into the mixture, then turned the food blender back on once more. After a few minutes Tariq was left with a slimy and rubbery solution. Taking this to the Concretonator's tank he added it to the remaining cement and olive oil slurry.

Ever the perfectionist, Tariq attached a DVD remote control to the Concretonator. He was certain the addition of the remote control would allow him to adjust the mixture, and the direction of the flow, as and when it was necessary.

The Concretonator was now, finally, ready.

Chapter 7.
Concretonator Away

"Dave," Tariq called up the stairs, "we're ready. Come down."

Oh no! Dave thought. "I'm on my way," he called back.

"I'm glad you're here," Tariq said. "I've finally sorted out all the problems. There's nothing for you to worry about now. Just go and stand in the cabinet, which I specially constructed, and you will be able to see that everything has been fixed."

"Fantastic," Dave replied, not meaning it one bit as he trundled himself off to the cabinet, and stepped into it.

The hole in the back of the cabinet had been repaired with a sheet of MDF, the medium density fibreboard being glued and nailed in place.

"Wait there, Dave. I'm adjusting the direction and force," Tariq said as he fiddled with the DVD remote controller, which was now the only way the machine could be controlled. The Concretonator's nozzle was moving left, then right, up, then down, in uncontrolled jerks, as Tariq pressed random buttons on the black control box.

"I'm ready, Dave," Tariq said as he beamed at the feather. Tariq was well pleased with the updates he'd made to the machine.

Dave paused. He'd seen how the Concretonator's nozzle had moved. He was very concerned.

"Are you all right, Dave?" Tariq asked.

He thought about his need to overcome the one thing that stopped him from being the person he wanted to be—the wind. Dave sighed and then nodded. "Yes," he said. As the words past his lips he knew, at that moment, this was likely to be his very last appearance in the new world he was just getting to know.

"Right," said Tariq, "Five, four, three, two, one, Concretonator away!" Tariq pressed the red button on the machine's newly added controller. The hose spewed out its contents and covered the lab's ceiling. Then, before it swung sideways and sprayed the shelves, the nozzle changed direction and sprayed the far end of the laboratory. Finally it stopped. Tariq mopped his brow, relieved.

Dave's eyes were wide open, as was his mouth. He couldn't believe what he'd just witnessed.

"Whoops!" said Tariq. "Wrong button. Sorry, Dave. I could never get the hang of these kind of controls." Dave frowned as Tariq told him of his issues with DVD controllers. "Just stay there," Tariq continued, "I'll get it right in a moment."

Dave stood still, and tried not to look worried. Tariq attempted to work out how the controller worked.

"Stay where you are. I think I've got the hang of it now," Tariq called across the lab: Dave stood statue-like in the old shower cabinet. As he stood there, gobsmacked, he tried to stop his knees from knocking just by thinking about it.

Tariq pressed a green button and the Concretonator took aim at a brave but reluctant feather. Within seconds a thick liquid splurged from the end of the machine's nozzle. It hurtled through the air at a very worried Dave.

Dave had already taken a deep breath as a precaution. He was certain he'd experience a repeat performance of Tariq's last test. But this time the gooey stream exerted almost no pressure on his body at all. Dave had been wrong.

Tariq was jumping around whooping with joy, albeit very slowly. This was a first—he'd actually made something that worked, and after all this time perhaps he could be like his grandfather Tarquin.

"This is absolutely tremendous," Tariq exclaimed joyously.

Dave looked down at his body; he was now covered in a thick slimy liquid which was extremely flexible, almost flexible enough not to cause any problems with his movement. He could move his arms, he could move his feet and he could look from side to side. Dave took one step out of the cubicle and after an initial resistance to gravity he fell flat on his face.

"Dave, are you okay? How are you feeling?" Tariq said as he made his way to his floor hugging friend.

"Probably yes, and very heavy," Dave replied to Tariq's questions.

"That's to be expected," Tariq answered. "Can you move?" he asked.

Dave tried to move his arm, and his arm did move fluently, but slowly, which was quite good for a feather, which was now completely covered in some kind of rubbery cement.

Dave tried moving his foot and he found it also moved. Dave tried to lift his head from the floor and he was able to do that as well, with only a little struggle.

Dave was surprised at how his new coating (or suit) was flexible enough to allow him to move, even though the mixture was naturally heavier than anything he'd been used to before.

"Right, Dave. It's clear you can move. But at this moment in time you are finding it a bit difficult. So I think you need some training," Tariq observed.

"Yeah. I think you're right," Dave said, as he struggled to stand up.

Dave's new shell suit was amazing, every direction he tried to move he could, albeit with some resistance. He would definitely need to do some serious training to wear the suit without issue. But he knew, now, his wind problem was over and he was pleased.

"Okay, Tariq, what do I do next?"

"I will create a training plan, a plan never devised before, a plan so specific it will eliminate the effects of your concrete suit, a plan that will..."

"I get it, Tariq. I do," Dave said as he interrupted his friend.

Tariq ignored Dave's interjection and continued. "A plan that will give you unknowable powers, and together we will get you used to your new shell suit. That okay?" Tariq said, finally.

Dave sighed. "Okay. Absolutely," he replied, feeling less worried than he had earlier, and very relieved he was still alive after Tariq's experiments. But he wasn't so sure about Tariq's view he'd get 'unknowable' powers by wearing the suit.

"Tremendous. We'll have some tea now. Then start training first thing tomorrow morning."

"Er! Okay, Tariq. One thing though. How do I get out of this suit?"

Chapter 8.
Enjoyable Exercise (not)

"Ding-a-ling-a-ling," said Tariq.

Dave sat up on the sofa and threw back the orange, green, yellow, red, and brown crocheted cover. He twisted left, then right, as he looked around Tariq's lounge. He could have sworn he'd heard someone attempting to sound like a bell; but no one was around.

"Ding-a-ling-a-ling," came the awful noise from a newly installed speaker. It had been attached to the wall next to the rug which covered the entrance to the laboratory.

Dave rolled his eyes. *Ah!* he said to himself. It was now obvious Tariq had fitted a speaker so he'd no need to shout up the stairs any longer. However, no matter how hard Dave thought about it, he couldn't figure out why on Earth Tariq had tried to imitate a bell.

As Dave made to leap off the sofa and make his way down into the lab, a twinge of pain shot through his arms and legs, and then his chest. At that moment he recalled the previous evening's events, and how his flexi-crete suit (as Tariq had named the flexible concrete suit) had been removed. Tariq had promised Dave that he'd think of a better way to remove the suit, the next time Dave would have to wear the wind-defeating flexi-crete overall. But, although it had taken a lot to convince Dave, the large hammer had been the only way.

"Ding-a-ling-a—," Tariq started again.

Dave made his way towards the rear of the hutch and pulled back the rug which covered the lab's entrance then yelled down the stairs. "I'm coming down, Tariq. Stop 'ding-a-linging'. It sounds rubbish. I'm just going to have a cup of tea first."

There was no answer from the basement laboratory, and the 'ding-a-linging' didn't happen again.

Dave put the kettle on.

Dave made his way down the stairs then pushed open the door into Tariq's Lab, and then stared at what was in front of him.

Tariq had set up a training circuit along the back wall of his underground laboratory. Dave couldn't imagine where Tariq had got all the different pieces of equipment from. There were bars on poles, bars on other bars, and then bars with huge brown looking discs at each end.

"Right, Dave. While you wear your flexi-crete suit you'll have to make your way around this training circuit. It'll help build up your strength—"

Dave started to speak before Tariq could finish. "A few things, Tariq."

"Yes?"

"I don't have my flexi-crete suit on—"

"Yes."

"And where did you get all this bar-stuff from? It wasn't here last night; at least I don't think it was."

"Most of it, I made, while you were asleep. I had a few bits and pieces lying around. The

Land Lord had some stuff he doesn't use, so I, sort of, borrowed it."

Dave nodded as he thought about his friend's answer. "Okay. I get that."

"Good," Tariq said. "All we need to do now is put your suit on. I say *we*, but really I mean you!" Tariq smiled at Dave.

"Oh! Have you figured out another way to remove the flexi-crete suit yet?"

Tariq paused. "Um," he said, then looked away and focused on one of the shelves on the opposite side of the lab.

"TARIQ!"

"Er," Tariq said. "Possibly," he added.

"POSSIBLY! You said you would. You promised."

"I know, Dave. I know. And I will."

"When?"

"Soon, Dave. Very soon." Tariq quickly changed the topic. "Shall we get you suited up then?"

Dave's mouth hung open.

"You never know when someone will need you," Tariq said. "It's for the best," Tariq added as he raised his eye brows, and smiled once again.

OMG! Dave thought. It was clear he'd no choice but to get the suit on, and then pray

Tariq would figure out a different way to remove it, once it was finished with.

Dave walked toward the old shower cabinet—the one that had been made specially. He shook his head as he stepped into it, then turned to face the nozzle.

For a change Tariq pressed the right sequence of buttons on the DVD remote controller, and within a few minutes Dave was wearing his flexi-crete suit.

"Okay. What's the next step?" Dave asked.

Tariq explained to Dave the idea behind a training circuit. "—and that's all you have to do," Tariq finished.

"What's the ding-a-linging for?"

"Oh! Er! I'm sure it's what happens in the human world before they start a training circuit."

Dave took a deep breath and looked at the training equipment, and then frowned. *What have I let myself in for now*? he wondered. There, in front of him, were benches, parallel bars and a treadmill. A climbing wall, ropes and a trampet. Dumbbells, a cross-walker and a static cycle.

Dave listened to Tariq's instructions, then, after a moment, he started the circuit. He walked across the benches, struggled across the parallel bars and ran on the treadmill.

Then he ran up and down the benches and heaved himself back across the parallel bars and jogged on the treadmill once again. With the circuit complete Tariq directed Dave to the climbing wall, and rope, and trampet. Once Dave had finished those circuits Tariq indicated the dumbbells, cross-walker and static cycle. Dave stared at Tariq and shook his head. Tariq just nodded. Dave sighed and continued the final circuit; or so he thought.

After one hundred circuits around the tortuous assault course Dave collapsed on the floor.

"Enough," Dave begged.

"Okay, Dave," Tariq said. "You can stop for five minutes. But I must say four hours isn't really enough."

"NOT ENOUGH?" Dave exclaimed.

"No, and for one reason only."

"That being?" Dave wheezed.

"That being the fact that you will, more likely than not, be wearing your tremendous flexi-crete suit for a lot longer than four hours, when you need it."

"Okay. I get your drift. How long then?" Dave said.

"I reckon, probably—another five days ought to do it," Tariq replied.

"ANOTHER FIVE DAYS?" Dave repeated, utterly stunned at Tariq's answer, and now very, very worried.

"Yep. That's how long," Tariq stated in his matter of fact tone.

Oh my God, Dave thought to himself. *I'm going to die. Really die!*

"Don't worry, Dave. You won't die," Tariq reassured him. "Trust me, I'm a tortoise."

Five days later an exhausted Dave begged breathlessly, "Can I have a cup of tea now?"

"Of course you can," Tariq said. "You've completed your training."

For one moment Dave was relieved. But then he realised it would now be time to remove the flexi-crete suit.

An idea popped into his head; he should do another few circuits. He couldn't bear the thought of the shell suit being removed in the manner it had been a week ago. As the thought rested in his head, he looked at the training equipment. The thought disappeared, instantly. There was no way on earth he could do any more. He nodded to himself; he knew he would have to face the large hammer once more.

"Okay, Tariq," he said. "I'm ready for the hammer."

"What!" Tariq replied. "No need, Dave. I've figured it out. I've figured out how to get you out of the suit." Tariq was beaming at Dave.

"That's great, Tariq. What do I need to do?"

"Put this in your mouth." Tariq handed Dave a gum shield to protect his teeth.

Dave took the piece of rubber, then stared at Tariq as he tried to work out what Tariq had in mind. "Put it in my mouth?"

Tariq nodded.

"How's that going to help me out of this suit?"

"I'm going to make it looser."

"How?"

"Dave! There's nothing to worry about. Trust me, I'm a tortoise."

Oh my word! Dave thought. For a minute he considered challenging his friend. Then he placed the gum shield in his mouth. "Moh kay. Wha do I nee to do now?"

"Nothing. Just stand there." Tariq made his way to some shelving in the darkest area of his lab. For many minutes Dave's tortoise friend vanished in the blackness. Then, as Dave gazed at where Tariq had disappeared, his tortoise friend reappeared. With him Tariq had a trolley, and on top of it was a rucksack and what seemed to be a life jacket which had been wrapped around a huge metal pole. And for some reason the device had a large pale yellow coloured tube attached to it.

Dave narrowed his eyes. He had no idea what Tariq was going to do with the peculiar equipment he was bringing.

"Okay. Ready," Tariq said.

"Wha?" Dave asked.

"You've got to put this rucksack on."

"Why?"

"Er! Just because?"

Dave pulled the gum shield from his mouth. "Tariq! Just tell me."

Tariq sighed. He didn't want to alarm his new friend. But he knew he had to tell him all the same. "I need to put this jack hammer in it."

"Jack hammer?"

"Yes. The thing with the huge tube."

"Oh! Is that all?"

Tariq frowned. "Er. Yes."

"Okay. That's all you needed to tell me." Dave shrugged as much as he could in his flexi-crete suit. Dave had no idea what a jack hammer was, he didn't know it was a machine workmen used to break up the ground, very loudly. Dave had only been around as an individual for less than a day.

However, he was about to find out everything he needed to know about jack hammers, very soon.

Dave put the gum shield back in his mouth. Tariq helped Dave into the rucksack, then put the jack hammer into the empty rucksack.

Tariq uncoiled the long pale yellow hose as he stepped away from his friend, and walked towards a huge air compressor, which was out of sight behind the shelving in the shadows. He attached the yellow pipe to the compressor. After a few moments thought he lifted a pair of ear mufflers from a hook on the wall next to the machine, and made his way back to Dave.

"Here," Tariq said as he thrust the woolly ear mufflers in Dave's direction."

Dave blinked. "Wha are hey or?" Dave mumbled. His gum shield still in place.

Tariq had to think for a moment. He didn't want to alarm Dave. "Erm. To stop your ears getting bits of the flexi-crete suit in them," Tariq replied, being honest, but not quite honest. For sure they would stop bits of the suit getting in Dave's ears, but they would also block out a lot of the noise the jack hammer would make.

"Hanks, Thariq." Dave took the mufflers and put them over his ears.

Tariq walked back to the air compressor, took one last look at Dave, turned his back, put his nose bungs in his ears, then pressed the on button. The jack hammer started up.

"Ta, ta, ta, ta, ta, ta, ta, ta, ta—rick," Dave exclaimed as he started to shake; A LOT.

"St, st, st, st, st, st, st, st—op," Dave tried to shout. Things were getting blurry as his eyeballs bounced up and down in his head. Then Dave felt a tingling along his arms and legs, and down his back; like something pulling away from his skin. *Oh no! I'm coming to bits*, he thought.

Tariq decided it was time to press the off button.

Dave's violent up and down motion tailed off.

Tariq turned back to look at Dave and noticed something odd. It seemed, that for some reason, Dave was still moving up and down, just less vigorously. Tariq wondered whether the flexi-crete suit had, somehow, trapped the jack hammer's movement because of the rubber it was made from. But as he continued to stare at Dave the strange feather slowed down and then stopped.

Dave struggled out of the rubberised concrete shell suit and, without saying a single word, stormed out of the lab back up to Tariq's kitchenette, and, before you could say, '*circuit training for five days non-stop is extremely exhausting*', Dave was sound asleep on Tariq's sofa yet again.

Chapter 9.
A New Problem

"Dave," Tariq said as he jumped up with glee. "I think I've found it!"

Dave who was still comatose on Tariq's sofa, came to, and opened his eyes. In an instant he became aware of the silent, but burning screams that came from the muscles in his arms and legs.

"What?" Dave said as he woke. He couldn't hear Tariq above the noise his muscles made. They'd been quite happy whilst Dave had slept. But now he was awake they made sure he knew, very well, what he'd put them through the day before. They had no idea it was actually all Tariq's fault.

"I've found it," Tariq repeated. He was sat at the kitchen table waiting for a pot of tea to brew.

"Found what?" Dave said, not at all interested. He had muscle problems to deal with. Even so, Dave swung his legs from the sofa and eased his feet to the floor.

"Your next adventure, Dave! The task your flexi-crete suit was designed to help you with," Tariq declared, ecstatic.

Dave sighed. He knew he was here for a reason, but the pain in his muscles was something else to overcome. "And what's that then?" Dave asked as he stood and carefully made his way into the kitchen. He pulled a chair back from under the kitchen table and then, very slowly, lowered himself down onto it.

"This—Have a look," Tariq showed Dave the two page feature in the most recent Daily Heron; the newspaper all of the area's animal community had delivered to their door.

Dave read the article. "What's that got to do with anything?" he said. "I mean it's only about the Emit family. And the fact they've been entered into the 'Guinness Book of Records'—whatever that it—for being the world's worst ever time keepers," Dave finished. He put the paper back down on the table and looked at his friend.

"Yes," Tariq agreed. "But don't you find their circumstances rather peculiar?"

Dave re-read the article. "What? The fact they don't have any jobs. The fact they've never been able to go on holiday. The fact their milk, which is delivered to their front door every day, has gone off by the time they pick it up from their doorstep?"

"Yes," Tariq said.

"No," Dave replied.

"Honestly, Dave? If there's nothing strange then surely they'd all be dead by now. And they look so reasonable," Tariq said as he looked at the Emit family picture on the second page of the Daily Heron feature. The picture consisted of Trevor Emit as he stood next to his wife, Daphne; they both looked confused. And, at their feet, was a very miserable looking dog. Tariq turned the newspaper back around so Dave could see the picture.

"Okay. Now you've said that, it does seem slightly strange," Dave agreed.

"I think this is a case for Brave Dave the Feather, and Tremendous Tariq the Tortoise;

the gifted tortoise that is," Tariq said feeling masterful.

Oh no! Dave sighed inwardly for the millionth time that day. "Okay. What do we do now?"

"Easy," Tariq replied. "We pack up and get to their house as soon as possible."

"That's a great idea," Dave said. "But what about my suit?"

Tariq looked at his friend and knew it was a good question. Tariq finished his cup of tea. "Come with me. Let's see what we can do." Tariq got up from the table and made his way back down the stairs to his lab. Dave followed.

Once again Tariq disappeared behind the huge shelves in the depths of the laboratory. Dave couldn't see how far back they went. Tariq's lab seemed huge. Dave couldn't imagine how long it had taken for Tariq to create the space under his hutch, but it must have taken quite a long while.

After what seemed to be a very long time, and lots of crashes and bangs, Tariq reappeared from the darkness, behind him he dragged a long black bag.

Dave looked at the bag, shocked. It was shaped just like a body, but not just any body—a human body!

Before Dave could say, '*Tariq. What have you done?*' Tariq had unzipped the bag and pulled out a mannequin. "Got this from a dress shop that was closing," he explained.

Dave sigh with relief. He seemed to be doing a lot of that lately. "What are you going to do with that?" Dave asked.

Tariq stood the shop dummy next to Dave. It was a lot taller than Dave.

From nowhere, it seemed, Tariq produced a saw. Dave's eyes almost popped from his head. But as Tariq started to cut the dummy down to Dave's size, Dave started to relax. He knew what Tariq was doing, and Dave was very happy.

Within minutes the mannequin matched Dave's height. Now cut down to size Tariq took the dummy and placed it in the specially constructed old shower cubicle.

Tariq turned to Dave and smiled. "We can create your suit—WITHOUT YOU IN IT!"

Dave nodded. He smiled as well.

"And," Tariq continued, "we can take it with us. How tremendous is that?"

"Very," Dave said, and Tariq turned on the Concretonator.

Chapter 10.
Blinkin' Dog

Dave and Tariq got their stuff ready and dumped Dave's flexi-crete shell suit onto a small trolley. There was no way Dave could wear the suit all the way to Trevor Emit's house, wherever that was. Even with all his training the suit would be too heavy; and Tariq knew it as well.

After phoning the *Daily Heron* Tariq had managed to get the newspaper to reveal the road the Emits lived in; but, unfortunately, not the house number.

For Tariq this was not a problem. They would go to the road, then take it from there. Tariq was sure the Emit family's house could be found without any issue. All they would need to do was spot a house with letters stuck in the letter box, and many milk bottles on the doorstep. At least, that was his plan.

And once there, Dave being *'Brave Dave the Feather, helper of all needful people'*, would fix Trevor Emit's problem, because that was what Dave did; he helped people.

As Dave pondered the Emit's problem he was not entirely sure that Trevor Emit, or his family, actually had a problem, but decided to go along with Tariq's idea just in case.

"Ready, Dave? Know what we're doing?" Tariq asked.

"I think so," Dave replied.

"Great," said Tariq, looking forward to sorting out Trevor Emit's problem with Dave, and being part of the adventure himself.

* * *

Tariq, happy in the knowledge he knew what they were doing, led Dave to the road. Dave followed. Behind him he dragged Tariq's trolley loaded up with his flexi-crete shell suit.

It was a tough journey. The couple needed to keep to the shadows as it was daylight. In some places there was no cover at all, and the two adventurers had to rush from one hedge to another so as not to be seen.

As they made their way along the roads, both failed to notice a big furry cat sitting in a tree; a cat that watched them intently. As it turned its head, to follow their progress, the morning sun glinted off its name tag and picked out the words 'my name is Slime'.

Slime not only watched them, Slime franticly scribbled notes into an old battered jotter.

* * *

After a while the two adventurers reached the Emit family's road. They stopped for a breather. In fact Tariq stopped because Dave was puffed out; he'd pulled the trolley all the way.

"Tariq," Dave said, grateful for the short break. "How will we find the right house?"

"Well," said Tariq, "I'm certain there will be something which will show us where the house is, and when that something happens we'll know."

"Like what?" Dave asked

Before Tariq could answer and tell Dave his thoughts about uncollected newspapers and multiple milk bottles, a shaggy, short, unkempt white and black spotted dog scampered out of a driveway, then skidded to a halt in front of them. It looked confused.

"Hi dog," Tariq said, and winked at Dave. Of course Tariq was only joking when he'd asked the dog, because he knew dogs couldn't understand people. One of the dog's eyes twitched nervously.

"Do you know where the Emit family's house is?" Tariq said as he continued his little joke. The dog blinked then flicked its head to one side and blinked again.

"Dave, I think this dog's got a nervous tic."

"That I have," answered the dog. It had heard Tariq's comment. All the while it continued to blink uncontrollably, and flick its head this way and that; occasionally it tried to scratch an ear with one of its rear legs.

"Dave, did you hear that?"

"What?" said Dave.

"'That I have'," Tariq repeated.

"Yep. Why? Didn't you?"

"Of course I did. But what was it?"

"The dog, you fool," Dave replied.

"Wow! A dog that talks," Tariq said.

"What's so amazing about a dog that talks?"

"It's a dog," said Tariq.

Dave, I think this dog's got a nervous tick

"Yeah, and you're a tortoise," Dave pointed out.

"So?" Tariq questioned.

"You talk," Dave said.

"Right! But it's a dog!" Tariq said again.

"I know. And you're a tortoise," Dave repeated.

"Are you trying to say I'm the same as a dog?" Tariq asked, a little put out by Dave's comment.

"No! Of course not, Tariq," Dave said. "But you are a quadruped. You are an animal with four legs."

"Right," said Tariq.

"Right," Dave said.

"Right—okay. Do you think there's any mileage in asking it where the Emits' house is?"

"I don't know," Dave said, then continued. "Why did you ask it in the first place then?"

"Because I thought it might point," Tariq replied.

"Point?" Dave asked, not sure what Tariq was trying to say.

"Yes. I can see that's not reasonable now. Especially as it can't stand still for one moment."

"Well," said Dave. "Ask it again, and see if you get an answer."

"Dog," said Tariq, addressing the dog once more, "do you know where the Emit family's home is?"

"I do know of the Emit family's home," the dog replied.

"That's tremendous," said Tariq. "Are you all right?" he continued. He was distracted by the dog's continual twitching.

"What do you mean?" said the dog.

"I mean, are you all right? You seem to have a problem," Tariq carried on.

"I don't have a problem. Do you?"

"No," Tariq responded quickly, not quite sure why he'd been asked.

"Why do you think I have a problem then?" the dog asked as it collapsed on the floor, then vigorously scratched its exposed stomach with its alternate rear leg, which wasn't quite enough so the remaining rear leg joined the first one in the scratching.

"Because you just can't keep still," Tariq replied, and added, "Actually, you cannot even keep upright."

"That's not me," the dog continued, getting up from the floor still blinking and twitching its head. "That's my tick. It's very nervous you see."

"No, not really," Tariq said.

"Well," said the dog, "I have this nervous tick."

"Yeah, I can see that."

"But you don't," said the dog.

"Yes I do," Tariq countered.

"No you don't," said the dog again.

I have a nervous tick, one you cannot see

"Okay, dog. Explain it to me," Tariq said as

he lifted his Deerstalker cap and scratched his head.

"I have a nervous tick. One you cannot see," the dog explained.

Tariq looked at Dave and shrugged his shoulders; he shook his head and smirked. How on earth could the dog say that he, Tariq, could not possibly see the nervous tic?

"But I can," Tariq said to the dog.

"No you can't," said the dog again, "I have a tick that's nervous."

"Eh?" Tariq said, very confused.

"The tick I have," the dog continued, "being a tick, an arthropod if you will, happens to be one of a nervous disposition.

It's the nervous disposition of the tick that makes me twitch."

"Ah! You have a tic," Tariq repeated still convinced that the dog was going on about a nervous affliction.

"Exactly," said the dog, in the belief the tortoise had finally got it.

"A tic that is not a twitch but an Arthur Pod," Tariq said as he attempted to understand, not daring to delve into a dictionary and make himself out to be uneducated, because he was. (Educated that is).

Anyway Arthur was certainly a stupid name for a pod especially as a pod was the name for a bunch of dolphins. What on earth was this dog trying to say? That it had a whole gang of dolphins roaming about its body and the gang's name was Arthur? How stupid!

"Got it in one," the dog replied, a bit happier.

"A tic that's nervous?" queried Tariq.

"Yes," said the dog.

"Why is it nervous?" Tariq asked.

"Don't ask me; ask it," the dog said.

"Where is it?" Tariq said, not knowing why because he could certainly see that the tic was all over the dog.

"If I knew that then do you really think I would allow it to stay about my person?" the dog questioned.

This question caught Tariq by surprise. As a frown crossed his brow, he turned to Dave. "Dave?" Tariq said, hoping for some help.

"Personally, I don't think a dog, in its right mind, would really want a tick on itself," Dave said.

"Right," said the dog. "Anything else you want to know?"

"Er. Yeah," said Tariq as he attempted to put the tick question out of his head.

"And what may that be?" said the dog.

"Do you know where the Emit family home is?" Tariq tried again.

"That I do," said the dog.

Oh my god. Tariq sighed to himself. *Why can't anyone give me a straight answer in the first place?* "Okay, dog. Where is it?" he asked.

The dog lifted one of its front legs, curled it under its body, and pointed its nose at the house Tariq and Dave were now standing in front of.

"Thank you, dog," said Tariq.

The dog wandered off in the direction of the Emits' house.

"Dog. Where are you going?" Tariq called after it.

"Home," said the dog.

"You live there?"

"Yes," said the dog, "I'm the Emit family pet."

"Tremendous!" Tariq said, exasperated.

Chapter 11.
The Observatory

"Dave, we're here," Tariq said in a hushed voice.

"I know that, Tariq. The dog just said so," Dave replied.

"Well? What do we do now? This is your specialist area."

"I think we need to sit and observe the situation. To see if we can get an angle on the problem we believe exists," Dave said, adding to himself, *'or at least the problem you believe exists'*. "But, before we sit down, we must find a place from which to make our observations." Dave cupped a hand to his mouth, then whispered in Tariq's ear, "Where we won't be seen."

Tariq half-closed his eyes and nodded knowingly. "Yes. Of course," he agreed.

Dave looked around the Emit family's front garden. A little way along from the cracked concrete path to the front of the pale-yellow house, he saw a small opening in the front garden's hedge. The hedge followed the low brick wall which separated the garden from the pavement and road beyond.

Dave wheeled his wooden trolley into the gap in the hedge, then signalled for Tariq to follow.

After he'd looked around to make sure he hadn't been observed, Tariq scurried over to join Dave in the hedge. They sat on the trolley and started their vigil; they watched, and waited, and observed. Both were keen to see what would happen next and then discover the source of the Emits' problem; if, in fact, there was a problem.

The hedge was clearly an evergreen, which helped them a lot; if the wind blew they wouldn't be exposed because of dropping leaves, as had happened with most of the trees in the area—autumn was in full swing.

Tariq turned to Dave and grinned. In a hushed voice he said, "This is exciting, isn't it?"

Dave smiled too. "I guess. I mean, as long as there's something we can sort out. And the Emits aren't just very lazy people."

"Do you think they could be?" Tariq asked. He'd not felt that, after he'd seen their photo in the Daily Heron, nor when he'd read their story. And the dog hadn't seemed lazy at all, the way it kept moving all the time.

Dave shrugged. "I like to believe in people, especially those that need real help.

Like the girls I helped the other day. How are

we to know?"

Tariq pursed his lips. He knew Dave was

right. "That's why we're doing this," he said.

Dave nodded. "We'll see," he said.

Little did either of them know what was

going to happen next.

Chapter 12.
Trevor Emit

Trevor Emit sat on his dark-green sofa, in his lounge, and smiled to himself. He couldn't wait for the post's arrival the next day. This was it! He would get the job he'd applied for, and, at long last, he would be employed. It would be the end of his terrible troubles.

The thin, tall, blonde ruffle-haired man took a swig from his coffee with sour milk. He adjusted his long orange and brown checked dressing gown. He'd got used to sour milk now; the little lumps of used-to-be milk no bother any longer. Even if the milk had bothered him nothing would stop him as he drunk the coffee. He was determined to be awake the next morning when his letter was pushed into his letter box, and the coffee would make sure he'd be awake.

All he had to do now was to wait for the letter to arrive. He would go to the front door, open the door, and take the letter from the wall-mounted box next to the door.

He would open the letter and it would say he'd got the job. It would be that simple. This time he would succeed, after all the years of trying. And he would succeed because he had a plan.

And perhaps his wife would be pleased. Daphne always said she believed in him, but how much longer would she wait? In fact, could she wait any longer?

Trevor was worried that the love of his life, his soul-mate, maybe at the end of her tether—not that she'd said as much. But Trevor new people had their limits, it was clear from all the jobs he'd applied for, only to be rejected because he was a little late for the interviews, mostly by no more than a few days.

He'd promised Daphne so much when they'd met. But he'd never been able to deliver on his promises. Especially when the promises required him to be at a certain place, at a certain time. This time it was just the front door, when the post was delivered. How hard could that be? Trevor wondered.

Poor dear Daphne. It wasn't as if he hadn't been to university, so jobs should have been easy to get. It was only the fact that, when he'd got to the exam room, to take the final exam, he'd found it empty; much like the lecture rooms he'd gone to during his terms at university.

Even more than that, the exam room doors were always locked; so it wasn't really his fault he'd not got his degree. It was more related to the fact the examinations were never on the days he'd turned up, and that wasn't for the want of trying.

This trouble, the trouble of not being on time had haunted him for a large part of his life. No matter how hard he'd tried, nothing had worked; being on time was something he'd never been able to achieve. Could lateness be genetic? He didn't know. But he certainly wished it were, because then he could blame it on his parents, whoever they had been; having been orphaned at a very young age he had no clue.

* * *

Trevor was very lucky to be married. It was only Daphne's belief in him that had allowed the marriage to go ahead.

When he hadn't turned up at the altar at the prescribed time, she had waited. Not only had she waited, she had waited three days. And when he'd finally got to the church, made his way along its grey flag-stone path through the graveyard, and made his way through the large crowd, which had gathered outside, Daphne had still been standing at the altar, still willing to marry him.

She hadn't cared about the other couples who'd been queuing up for the previous three days, nor their guests, she'd just believed in him; Trevor Emit.

But things were different now; it was six years later; six years of being married to the worst ever time keeper in history.

So bad was he that he now had an entry in the '*Guinness Book of Records*', an entry under the most un-praiseworthy title of '*The World's Worst Ever Time Keeper*'.

Trevor had to do something. He didn't know what, as he believed he'd tried every trick in the book; every single trick to make sure he was on time—to be where he was meant to be, when he was meant to be.

But it never worked. However, he had faith, and it was this faith in himself that had kept him going. How much longer it would keep Daphne going he had no idea.

Trevor took another swig from his lumpy-milk coffee and imagined what it would be like to have a job.

Chapter 13.
Morning Was Broken and Goggle

Morning was breaking and it was 7:14 a.m. Dave opened his eyes and stretched; he'd been roused by the *click, click, click* of a bicycle freewheeling. It was the postman. Tariq was somewhere in his shell doing things, and Dave did not bother to disturb him.

The postman rested his bike against the front wall of the house, against the hedge that hid Dave and Tariq from casual observers. The postman walked along the garden's cracked and chipped concrete path to the front door.

He plunged his hand into his postbag and pulled out a single letter, then pushed it into the letter box. It was one of those letter boxes which attached to the front of the house. One that required the owners of the house to leave their front door and collect their post from the box on the wall.

The postman about faced, walked back down the cracked pathway and got back on his bike, then headed for the next address which required a delivery.

* * *

Trevor was woken from another strange dream about time pieces, clocks and other such things by his radio alarm. As he opened his eyes the dream began to fade away. As usual he was left with a feeling of almost understanding. This was one of the most frustrating things about waking up. He could never grasp what it was he was meant to understand. He shrugged off the feeling, once again, and got up. Then a frown passed from one eyebrow to another. He'd got out of his bed! The last thing he remembered was drinking coffee with lumpy milk, in his lounge. How he'd got to bed was a mystery.

Like he did every time something strange happened he assumed his memory was at fault. But this time with less conviction. Trevor felt in his heart of hearts something was different, something had happened this time. But he still didn't know what.

* * *

Outside, hidden in the hedge, Dave heard a quiet *thud, thud, thud*. He guessed it was Trevor coming down the stairs to collect his mail.

The dog, the one Dave and Tariq had encountered the day before, appeared from the back of the house. It stood in the middle of the front garden.

It seemed to Dave that the dog had some interest in whether Trevor would manage to get his letter or not.

The instant Trevor reached the bottom of his staircase a thickness took hold; a dampening of worldly actions—all sorts of things slowing.

As the thickness extended to the immediate area, which included Dave's hedge, a strangely dressed individual popped out from the small drain at the front of the Emits' house.

The dog started to twitch and shake, as if its tick had started the world's first ever Jive dance contest for arthropods on a mammal, which was crazy because arthropods had been doing these competitions for years.

The individual was short, no more than 30 centimetres

The individual was short, no more than about 30 centimetres, dressed in green woollen clothing and wearing a floppy pointy green hat. Over its green jerkin it wore a deep maroon waist coat. In its hands, it held, what could only be described as a square, mahogany frame, not much larger than itself. Its face was of an apple green colour, and its chin was, what could only be called, pointy. It also had two pointed green ears, which stuck up either side of its hat, and left one in no doubt it was related to the faerie folk called goblins.

Dave was astounded by the appearance of the strange green man, but was even more astounded by what happened next.

Just as Trevor opened the front door to his house, the goblin held up its wooden frame to the front door. At that moment each side of the frame stretched until it matched the size of the house's door frame.

The view through the newly sized frame went all wobbly. It was as if Trevor was now being seen through the surface of a murky-green watery pool; one which had just had a stone thrown into it; ripples moved from the centre of the frame to its edges.

Dave continued to be astounded. All of a sudden the morning bird calls stopped. Then the sun zipped across the sky, faster than you could undo a pair of jeans, to take up its mid-afternoon position for the time of year.

Trevor unlocked his letter box and removed the letter. He was oblivious to what had happened. As far as he was concerned he'd got up and stepped outside to open his letter box.

He opened the letter, read it, looked at his watch, and sighed heavily. "No, no, no," Trevor moaned, "I was here, I got up at the right time. The letter says I can start work at

10:15 a.m., for my first day. Nooooo," he finished.

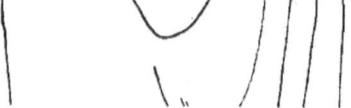

Trevor unlocked his letter box and removed the letter

"What time do you make it, Tariq?" Dave whispered into Tariq's shell.

"About 2 p.m. Why?" came Tariq's echoing reply.

"No reason." Dave turned back towards the house. A phone in the house had started to ring. The green goblin had vanished and so had the dog.

Trevor walked back indoors and picked up the phone.

"Mr Emit," the phone said.

"Yes?" said Trevor.

"Don't bother coming in. You're fired."

Click, went the phone.

Trevor looked at the handset momentarily; then his shoulders slumped and he hung his head. Slowly he replaced the phone's receiver, miserable and dejected.

"I don't know why I ever bother getting my hopes up," Trevor said to no one in particular. He closed his front door against a world that had dealt him yet another blow, in a long set of body blows.

* * *

Dave spent the rest of the afternoon pondering over Mr Emit's problem. Nothing much else happened apart from a few muted yells coming from the house, followed by statements such as, "I've burnt the bloomin' potatoes again." Which were promptly followed by responses like, "Don't worry, darling. I'll do some more." Apart from that, the house was quiet and there was no sign of the strange and short green man.

"I think Mr Emit has a problem," Dave said finally.

"I know that," said Tariq as he popped his head out of his shell. "That's why we're here isn't it?" Tariq frowned for a moment as he realised Dave had discovered something. "What, exactly, is Mr Emit's problem?" he asked.

"Ah! Well! That's quite difficult to explain. But, in essence, I feel it's got a lot to do with time frames," Dave said. "One thing's for sure though, we'll not be able to do anything about it today."

"How come?" asked Tariq.

"We need to do some research and find out more about this. This is not a case of your everyday wannabe poltergeist," Dave said referring to the problem of the missing school books he'd solved the other day. "Time to go back to your hutch I think," Dave finished.

It was now 6:21 p.m., the sun had just set, and Dave, with his trolley plus Tariq, made his way back to Tariq's hutch in the deepening twilight.

When they got back to the hutch Dave plonked himself down on Tariq's sofa, and Tariq put the kettle on to make a pot of tea.

"Do you have a book on genealogy?" Dave asked Tariq.

"I think so. But why do you want a book on denim? Do you have a cunning plan where we create some kind of cotton travelling machine or perhaps a swing or even a wig?"

"No! No! No! I need to find out about Mr Trevor Emit's family tree," said Dave.

"Sorry, I thought you were asking about blue cotton clothing or something."

"I really don't know how you manage to achieve anything, Tariq! Genealogy not jeanieology you idiot," Dave laughed.

"Ah! Well! That's something completely different. And I don't think I do. You could try using Goggle."

"Goggle?" Dave queried.

"Yeah, Goggle," said Tariq. "It's the *Internet search engine that surfs the information sea with clarity*'," Tariq said, quoting the website's marketing phrase; '*A search engine that will see exactly what you need to know.*'

"Internet? Search Engine? What *are* you going on about, Tariq?" Dave asked, very curious about these new things he'd not heard of before.

"Well, perhaps I do know stuff then," Tariq said, feeling rather pleased with himself.

"What is the Internet? And what on earth is a Search Engine?"

"Don't worry, Dave. I'll show you."

Tariq walked across his hutch and pressed a concealed button on the side of an old mahogany, Edwardian writing desk. Although battered in appearance the desk front opened up, and a computer keyboard slld out on a pair of black rails. The top of the writing desk opened and flicked backward, a small screen rose silently up from within.

"This is my secret connection to the entire world," Tariq said.

"Wow," said Dave agog. "What's that?"

"It's a computer terminal. A terminal that allows me to look up things I don't have books about."

"Okay, barring the fact I have no clue as to what a computer terminal is, you've got me interested. Show me what it can do," Dave said.

"Ask me something—anything," Tariq said.

"Okay. What is the base of the natural logarithm 'e'?" Dave smiled to himself knowing there was no way Goggle the

'*Internet search engine that surfs the information sea with clarity*' could know this. And there was definitely no way Tariq would know this either.

In a short moment after tapping away at the keys of his computer terminal Tariq said, "2.71828182845904523560 blah, blah, blah."

"Blinkin' flip," Dave swore, absolutely stunned. His mouth jabbered silently in awe. "Right. Right! Right," Dave eventually continued still not able to get over the power at Tariq's finger tips. This could be an extremely useful research tool, he thought.

Chapter 14.
Lettuce Custard

"Okay, Dave, where do we go from here?" asked Tariq.

"Well. I think there are a few essentials we need to know, before we can have any hope of helping the Emits; especially poor old Trevor," Dave said.

"Like what?" Tariq was intrigued.

"Well, firstly, we need to know what that little green man was about. That goblin," Dave said.

"Goblin?" Tariq queried. He was sure he didn't want to have anything to do with goblins. "Do they actually exist?"

"Before today, Tariq, I would have said not. And secondly Trevor's family history is something else, and thirdly, what happened to the morning?"

"Anyway, what little green man, or goblin as you call it?" Tariq said not recalling any little green man at all.

"Oh!—Yeah! I forgot," Dave said. "What *were* you doing in your shell this morning anyway?"

"Ah! That is a question. I'm not sure I can tell you. It's a secret." But Tariq being Tariq couldn't keep it to himself. "I've started developing the most excellent culinary addition to my hot 'n' soggy lettuce soup main course..."

"Good for you, Tariq," Dave interjected. "Can you tell me what it is?"

"I shouldn't. Especially as I've not got anywhere near completing the recipe. But as it's you I'll tell you—lettuce custard! How cool is that?"

"Lettuce custard!" Dave repeated trying not to feel ill, or give away any sign he thought it was probably the second most stupidest idea Tariq had come up with so far.

Tariq's hot 'n' soggy lettuce soup with microwaved bread being the first.

"That's right," Tariq said and smiled. The way Dave had been surprised by his revelation told him he'd hit on a really tremendous idea for a new dessert. "I'm just figuring out how to cook beetroot, so it can be added as a topping. But haven't quite got it right yet."

"That's good," said Dave, meaning it was good that Tariq hadn't got around to finishing what could only be called the most awful recipe on earth.

Dave hoped Tariq would never get around to finishing it. He knew, once it was finished what would happen, and the thought was not a pleasant one. Dave shuddered. There was no way he'd be able to get out of it. Once Tariq had finished his creation Dave knew he'd be the one who had to try it.

"Anyway," Tariq continued, "enough of my most tremendous cooking. What little green man?"

Dave almost choked, but hid it well. "Er, while you were working on your new recipe a little green man popped out of the drain. He had a wooden frame and somehow moved time forward approximately five hours forty-six minutes and thirty-three seconds," Dave said.

"No! Really? You've got to be joking." Tariq found it hard to believe what he was being told.

"No. I'm not. And this is exactly why we need to do some proper research."

"Why? Because getting beetroot to be a good topping takes an incredible amount of in-depth knowledge about root vegetables?" Tariq said.

"NO!" Dave said exasperated. He couldn't understand how Tariq had got back onto the recipe. "Research about the goblin, Tariq. It's important simply because little green men from drains are not an everyday occurrence. Or are they?"

Tariq shook his head. "Er. No. I don't think so," he said.

Dave nodded. "So this can only mean one thing; it means something really odd is going on. Will you please focus on the Emit family's problem. This is important. You thought this was important in the beginning. And now I agree. No more cooking stuff. Okay?"

"Okay, Okay! Don't lose your fancy yellow Lycra over-garment about it," Tariq said. "But it's a tremendous recipe, don't you think?"

Dave rolled his eyes.

Chapter 15.
Little Green Man

"Tariq, what does Goggle say about little green men and floppy caps?"

Tariq typed the question into Goggle and pressed the enter key. Within seconds the result was displayed. "Dave," he said, "we've got a result."

"Excellent!" Dave said.

"Might not be what you're after," Tariq said.

Dave shook his head. He knew how powerful this thing was, this 'Search Engine'. For a fact he'd tested it. "What does it say?" he asked. He couldn't wait to hear yet another perfect result from this most ingenious invention called a 'Search Engine'.

Tariq started to read out the results of Dave's question. "It says:," Tariq began, "'*Bombay, India. 1917. Informal group portrait of Australian troops, possibly a reinforcement for the 1st Wireless Signal Squadron, Mesopotamian Expeditionary Force, relaxing in the water.*' Does that help?"

"What! How can that possibly help? 'Bombay, India'! I knew it; this Goggle is not all it's cracked up to be. 'Wireless Signal Squadron' indeed!"

"I don't know why you asked me to use Goggle anyway," Tariq responded, "I'm sure I've got an old book on little green men and such things."

"Well! Thanks for letting me know that, Tariq. Could have saved some time. We need to sort out Trevor's problem as soon as possible. He's not in a good place. Where's the book?"

"It's over there on that shelf." Tariq pointed to a dusty bookcase stood against the wall next to the stairway down to the lab beneath his hutch. "It's called, '*The Guild of Gaia's Who's Who of Magical Beings*'. I think it'll cover what you're after," Tariq added.

Dave walked across Tariq's lounge to the bookshelf, then lifted a very large, heavy and dusty book from its middle shelf. He opened it up. After a few minutes of flicking through the pages Dave came across a picture he recognised.

"That's it, Tariq! The goblin is a Time Goblin! Well done that tortoise. Sometimes the junk you collect really does do the business!"

At last Dave began to feel some hope for poor old Trevor Emit, and himself. Now he had the book, the prospect of solving the riddle of the little green man, was now on the cards—something he'd be able to achieve. Things were beginning to look up.

"What's a Time Goblin when it's in a drain?" Tariq asked.

"Right. According to the book. A Time Goblin is '*a mythical being brought to life after the creation of Elves from the earth. After the Elves were made the remnants left over were used to create the Time Goblins.*' Apparently, because they were made from what was left over after the Elves had been created, they have hated the Elves forever. But, even more importantly, they also have a special hatred of mankind, mainly because mankind was the first creature to be created from the earth. It also says that, '*Time Goblins were given certain powers*' one of those powers being '*the power to control time to compensate them for their outrage about how they were brought into being*'. And '*as part of their Quadalveus*', which is basically their magic toolbox, they were given '*An Emar-Femit*' which, roughly speaking, is a wooden frame which can control time but only on a localised basis: This is amazing, Tariq!"

Dave was happy now they'd discovered the nature of the green individual. But one question still remained; why was the Time Goblin hassling poor old Trevor Emit in particular? To delve into this mystery Dave had to understand Trevor Emit's past.

"Tariq, do you have a book on genealogy? And I don't mean a book of cloth swatches, okay?"

"No."

"Oh! How am I going to finish this research then?"

Tariq paused before he replied, "Goggle?" he offered.

"Okay. I suppose Goggle's our only option then," Dave said.

"Let me know what you want to know, Dave."

"The Emit family tree," Dave said.

Tariq started to type away at his computer terminal. After a few exclamations of 'no', 'not this one', 'nope', Tariq finally said, "I think I've got it." He turned to Dave, "Have a look at this. I've found an Internet site called   '*www.extremely-ancient-family-trees.org*'. I think this will do the trick, mainly because it's very old."

"How can you tell that?"

"Well, apart from the download times, which I must say are extremely slow, just have a look for yourself."

"Wow!" Dave said as he looked at the site displayed on Tariq's computer terminal. "That does look really old," he said. Dave was astounded by the ever-so-visible cobwebs which covered the site.

"Yep. It certainly is," Tariq agreed.

"What do you do now?"

Tariq lifted an arm and brushed the cobwebs from the site. "There! Look!" he said as he pointed. "There's a place for names to be typed in. I can enter the family name we want to research."

"Okay," Dave said. "Enter '*Woods*'."

"What? Why? What's that got to do with anything?"

"Nothing," Dave said and smiled. "I was just making sure you're on the case. Enter '*Emit*'."

Tariq typed '*Emit*' into the site's search then pressed the enter key on his computer keyboard. The search results spoke for themselves.

"This is truly amazing, Tariq. These entries go back hundreds of years!"

Each of the results displayed, on the site's home page, was a link to other web pages, all of which were related to one, or another, aspect of the Emit family history.

Tariq clicked on each link in the list. In turn various details of the Emit family's history were displayed on the screen of Tariq's computer terminal.

After going through each and every link Dave said, "I think we now have an idea of how we can sort out Trevor Emit's problem. Tomorrow we'll begin."

Tariq turned to his friend. "This is tremendous," he said and grinned.

"Can't agree with you more," Dave said. He smiled as well. Good things were about to start, he hoped—especially for Trevor Emit and his family.

Chapter 16.
Smelly Air

For a moment Dave thought he was beneath the water once again as he struggled to breathe.

Within seconds he woke and the water dream faded. But he knew something was really wrong.

Dave sat up on the sofa and threw off his duvet. He looked around for Tariq, but his tortoise friend was nowhere to be seen; in fact Dave couldn't see anything because of the presence of a strange, very thick, and very smelly fog. Something that had totally filled the room.

The other reason Tariq couldn't be found, Dave realised, was because his friend wasn't actually in the room. And although Dave couldn't see anything in the room, he most certainly couldn't hear any Tariq-like noises either; and Tariq was never quiet, even when he needed to be.

Dave coughed and took a handkerchief from his pocket then placed it over his mouth. The smelly fog was truly smelly; a mixture of boiled dry cabbage, old fish carcasses, and burnt potatoes. Dave covered his nose as well. He hoped it would stop his stomach churning.

He stood up from the sofa—his makeshift bed—and noticed the fog was thicker towards the back of Tariq's hutch.

Dave decided the peculiar and smelly fog must be coming from the stairs that led down to Tariq's lab.

Before going to investigate Dave tied the handkerchief around his nose and mouth, and hoped it would block out the awful smell which drifted through the air. It didn't. Dave shook his head. He pulled another handkerchief from his pocket and tied it around his mouth and nose as well. Although not quite working, the smell had diminished enough to allow him to investigate what on earth Tariq was up to with his awful smells.

Step by step he made his way towards the door at the back of the hutch, his hands held out in front of him. He wanted to avoid cracking his nose or stubbing his toe on the back wall. He had an idea that it could be rather painful if he did.

His plan worked. Dave felt his hand connect with the rug which covered the secret door to the lab below. He grabbed the rug and pulled it back, then stood aside as more smelly fog billowed out from the stairwell.

"Tariq?" he called down the stairs. His voice was muffled, the handkerchiefs tied around his face quietening his call. No matter, he thought. He would just call louder as he, definitely, wasn't going to take off the handkerchiefs and suffer the sick-making, belly retching smell again.

He got no reply. Dave started to worry. Tariq's lack of response concerned him a lot. He wondered whether the genius tortoise had finally made an invention that had beaten him.

Dave started down the stairs. The stairwell's dim light turned the smelly, thick fog, a light yellow colour.

"Tariq?" Dave called out again as he took a few more steps down into the yellowy nothingness.

"Ah *dare* you are, Dave," Tariq said as he saw his friend stick his head through the doorway into the lab. "How's it going?" he asked.

Dave was relieved but still wanted to know what was going on. "What on earth is this awful fog?" he said to his genius tortoise friend.

"I like your handkerchief," Tariq replied. "No! Handkerchiefs," he added. Tariq didn't really want to talk about the fog. "Is that going to be *bart* of your *suber* hero look?"

"No! And I'm not a super hero, Tariq. What is this fog?" Dave asked again.

Tariq knew his friend would not stop asking until he was told. "It's okay. No *beed* to worry, Dave. I've just *hab by* first go at creating lettuce custard. But I *haben't* quite got it right yet," Tariq said.

"You can say that again," Dave agreed. "Is there any way you can get some fresh air in here?"

"Why would I *wad* to do that?" Tariq replied.

"Because it stinks, actually it more than stinks, it reeks. No! No. Reeks doesn't come anywhere near describing this smell. I don't think there is a word that could come anywhere near to describing it."

"Can't say I *doticed*," Tariq said.

"Not *doticed*? Have you got a cold or something?" Dave asked.

"*Doe*," Tariq replied, "I usually put a couple of *bees* up my *dose* before I start *exberimenting* with *recibes*," Tariq showed Dave a spare set of tortoise nose bungs.

"And today?"

"*Yeb!*" Tariq confirmed.

"Blimey, Tariq. Get some fresh air in here now." Dave rolled his eyes and thought, *what is it with this tortoise?*

Tariq walked over to his work bench and pressed a bright yellow button. The fog started to disappear into a small hole at the back of the lab.

"What's that?" Dave asked.

Tariq removed his nose bungs. "It's an extractor fan, Dave."

"Why didn't you use that before?"

"Didn't want the noise to wake you," Tariq said.

"Did you ever think about the smell?" said Dave.

"What smell?" Tariq replied.

Dave sighed.

Chapter 17.
The Problem with Time Goblins

"Come on Tariq, we really ought to get ready. I'd prefer to be at the Emits' place before dawn breaks."

It was still early in the morning. Tariq's disaster with the Lettuce Custard had woken Dave around 5:30 a.m. Sunrise was not due for another couple of hours.

Dave loaded his flexi-crete suit onto Tariq's trolley once more, and, as an afterthought, retrieved 'The Guild of Gaia's,

Who's who of Magical Beings' and threw it onto the trolley as well.

Tariq picked up his satchel, stuffed a few bits and pieces into it, then slung it over his shoulder. "Okay, Dave, I think I'm ready. Are you?"

"Yep. I believe so."

Dave and Tariq made their way out of Tariq's pen and onto the road in front of the Land Lords' house. As they travelled they made sure they kept to the shadows, sneaking behind bushes and hedges, ducking behind cars and trucks, and sometimes just standing completely still. Very soon they arrived at the Emits' house unobserved.

"Tariq, I think we need to make camp where we were yesterday. Once we're done we'll work out a plan of action."

"Great, I like action," Tariq said, as he tried not to show his apprehension, and the fact that action was the last thing he wanted.

He'd never ever done anything brave before, apart from investigating the noise which had marked Dave's arrival in his pen a few days previously. This time it was different, this time he was not in his pen, and this time his hutch was a long way away, if things got a little scary.

"What's that knocking, Tariq?" Dave asked.

"Don't know, Dave," said Tariq.

"It's your knees," Shell said to Tariq, for once not speaking out loud for all the world to hear.

Oh good grief, Tariq sighed to himself.

"What fleas, Tariq? I don't have any fleas," Dave said not having any idea what Tariq was going on about.

"No, I said, I thought it might be the trees."

"I suppose it could be," Dave agreed. The weather, although pleasant, had a lot of wind.

Phew! Tariq thought, then whispered quietly, "Shell, keep your big mouth shut will you?" There was no response from Shell.

Dave and Tariq made camp under the hedge once again.

"What do we do now?" Tariq asked.

"Well, from the information we found out in the book, and the interesting net..."

"Internet," Tariq corrected.

"Okay, the Internet," Dave said as he corrected himself. "It seems the Emit family and the Time Goblins have been battling each other for all time. As far as I can work out the Emits, or at least, the Emit family line, are here to defend normal time; to make sure that summer changes to autumn and autumn to winter and one year to another, et cetera, et cetera.

"But the Time Goblins were given the ability to change time," Dave continued as he relayed what he'd read in Tariq's book. "In a small way, it was supposedly for the good. Because if everything happens when it should, then things would become so tedious all living things would just give up and simply die of pure boredom.

"So you have the Emits, and Trevor is just one of many throughout the world, a Time Guardian of sorts, and you have the Time Goblins. The *'Yin and Yang'* of time. A balance, not quite between good and evil, but more like between late and punctual."

"I see," Tariq said. "I think I know what you mean; every year when the 'Tortoise Tall Story Talkathon' is on, it's meant to start at 8:00 p.m., but no one actually turns up at that time. It's not until about 8:15 p.m. when they start to arrive. And no one is actually late; it's more like they are on time."

"Exactly," said Dave.

"And this is due to the Time Goblins getting the better of the Emits?" Tariq said checking he'd understood everything he'd been told so far.

"As I understand it, Tariq, yes. But why Trevor has his problem I don't know. I'm sure his mum and dad knew their responsibilities, and they must have brought him up to be a Time Guardian as much as they were."

"Strange," Tariq agreed, as he pretended to think about what Dave had described.

"Yes. It is strange. We need to find out more, and to do this we need to get into the Emits' house."

"But he's in there with his wife!" Tariq was getting seriously worried.

"I know, but I think there is a solution to that," Dave said and started to whistle. Tariq looked at Dave utterly dumbfounded.

KERLICK, CLICK, CLICK, CLICK, CLICK, CLICK.

The Emits' dog skittered around the corner of the house, its toe nails tapping on the path as it went.

"Oh! It's you again," said the dog.

"Yep. It's us," Dave replied as he stepped out from beneath the hedge. Tariq followed.

"What do you want?" the dog asked.

"I want to help you," Dave said.

"Help me?" the dog said as it started to twitch again. Once more it flicked its head this way and that. "What do I need help for?" the dog asked, incensed by the suggestion.

"Well. I want to help you with your nervous tick," Dave said.

"Do I really have to go over all that again?" Without waiting for a reply the dog turned around and started to make its way back to the rear of the house.

"Hold on," Dave said quickly. "It's not strictly help for you. More like help for your tick."

"Help the tick?" the dog queried unable to believe what it was hearing. "I don't think that, that tick needs any help, thank you very much! It's more than capable of giving me grief without any help from someone else."

"No," said Dave, "I agree. But to help it not to be so nervous any longer," he explained.

"And how might you do that then?" the dog asked, he was curious now.

"Well. I think I've worked out why it's so nervous."

The dog blinked, paused for a moment, then walked over to Dave; Dave explained his theories. He then told the dog what he wanted it to do.

"Your explanation is pretty far-fetched, young feather-me-lad," said the dog. "Actually downright ludicrous, laughable to say the least. But as I don't have a feather's chance in a tornado to get this sorted out any other way, I'll do as you ask.

"Even if this doesn't work I suppose I'm no worse off anyway." With this final comment the dog skittered back to the house.

"Tariq, get back under the hedge and get your stuff ready," Dave said.

"What's going on, Dave?"

"Wait and see," he replied.

A few moments later Dave and Tariq heard the muffled sounds of the Emits as they talked about the dog in their bedroom.

* * *

"Trevor, I think the dog wants to go out," Daphne said.

"Er?" said Trevor, half asleep.

"The dog wants to go for a walk," his wife said once more.

Trevor looked at the clock next to the bed.

"Daphne. It can't. It's only six in the morning," Trevor moaned.

"I really think it needs to go for a walk. Look at it."

Trevor looked at the dog. The dog was running around in circles, at the end of their bed, and as it chased its tail, occasionally, it fell over.

"Yeah, I think you're right," Trevor said, and frowned at the dog's strange new behaviour. He got out of bed, changed, and started to wander down the stairs.

"Come on, boy," Trevor called to the dog. "We're going for a walk."

The dog sat down in the Emits' bedroom and looked at Daphne with its puppy eyes.

"Come on, boy," Trevor called again as he walked back up the stairs and back into the bedroom. He bent over and leant nearer the dog. "Come on, boy," he whispered and clapped his hands on his thighs.

The dog didn't move.

Daphne pointed to herself and said, "Me as well?"

The dog nodded.

"Trevor, I think it wants me to come as well."

"What has got into this dog? It's never behaved like this before," Trevor said very confused.

"I don't know, Trevor, but even though it's early perhaps it would be nice, just this once, to go out before everyone else in the world is up."

Trevor smiled and nodded. He knew his wife was right.

Daphne got ready.

The dog jumped around and wagged its tail eagerly. The Emits, now ready, took their dog for a walk.

Chapter 18.
Dog Flaps and Clocks

"Nice one, Dave. How on earth did you do that?" Tariq said as he watched the Emits leave their house, with their dog in tow.

"Oh, don't worry about that," Dave said. To himself, he added, *I just hope I'm right.*

The Emits walked down the road and were soon out of sight. After double-checking the surrounding area Dave and Tariq left their hideaway.

Now they had the task of finding a way into the Emits' home. Dave hoped it would be a simple mission.

He glanced around to check to see that no one else was out and about. Satisfied, he beckoned Tariq to follow.

The two friends snuck along the hedgerow they'd been hidden in. The cover of the long shadows cast by the barely risen sun concealed their progress. The front lawn was draped in a thin veil of dew. Then the hedge ended. A wooden fence, the type made of wood-beige panels with joining fence posts, led towards the back of the Emits' house and the rest of the rear of the property.

As they walked down the path Dave glanced at the side wall of the Emits' semi-detached home. It was painted in a hotchpotch of pastel colours; pale yellows, pale blues, and even an attempt at pale pink. And next to the side of the house, all the way along the path, were many tins of different coloured paints. But by the look of their contents each and every one was about three-quarters full, and solid—dried out.

Dave wondered whether Trevor had started to paint the side of the house, then decided to go in for a cup of tea, then never managed to get back in time before the paint had hardened into a colourful cylinder no use to anyone.

Dave shook his head, and not for the first time. He felt truly sorry for the Time Guardian, who never knew he was one. And now Dave was even more determined to help Trevor Emit, and his family, and their dog.

Once they'd got around to the back of the house Dave recognised the usual see-through flap. Something he'd seen at the back of all the other houses he'd visited so far. This new world seemed to be full of houses with see-through flaps.

At least his hoped for wishes had been answered. In this case the flap was a lot larger than the last one he'd come across at the girls' house the other day. Dave nodded to himself and smiled. At least there was a way in.

"We go in through here," Dave said as he pointed out the flap to Tariq.

"Through there?" Tariq repeated. "Are you sure?"

"Of course I am," Dave said.

"Okay. If you insist," Tariq said, a lot more worried than he'd been throughout this latest of Dave's adventures.

Dave and Tariq heaved themselves through the flap and landed in a room full of smaller doors.

"Ah!" Tariq said. "Looks like we're in the kitchen."

"The kitchen? Yes! I suppose it is, but very much larger. Thanks, Tariq. You've made things a bit clearer."

Dave noticed the clock on the oven and said to himself, *Ah! There's one.*

"What do we do now then, Dave?"

"Well, as I see it, we need to remove every single clock in the house. Anything that has got to do with telling the time—has got to go."

"What for?" Tariq asked.

Dave decided it was time to reveal the conclusions of his research into the Emit family history. "Because Trevor Emit is a Time Guardian. Instead of looking after time he has decided to be ruled by it. I don't know why yet, something in this house may tell us. But, anyway, Trevor just does not know he should be looking after time and not being ruled by it."

"Oh!" Tariq said, "A Time Guardian?" the tortoise queried his friend.

"Yes. And the Time Goblin, who lives in his drain, is stopping him from doing his job. Which, strangely, is exactly what the Time Goblin should be doing. But because Trevor doesn't know what he should be doing, because he doesn't know he's a Time

Guardian, the Time Goblin is winning every time."

"Why doesn't Mr Emit know he's a Time Guardian?" Tariq asked.

"Good question, Tariq. Probably a very sad story. No time to discuss it now. Perhaps later."

"Right," Tariq said, although not fully understanding the outcome of a Time Guardian ignoring their responsibilities.

"And it is this one and only fact that unbalances the time continuum—the future and past history—around here. And much more importantly around Trevor's own time line.

"For us to undo this imbalance we need to remove everything Trevor relies on to tell the time."

"But why is that? It doesn't make sense," Tariq said.

"Simple, Tariq. A Time Guardian has to rely on their own sense of time; the internal clock which drives their ability to know when time is being changed. I'll give you an example. What's the time, Tariq?"

Tariq lifted his watch chain from his pocket and removed his timepiece. Tariq smiled. "That's simple, Dave. It's 6:15 a.m."

"Exactly," said Dave. "There you go. The first thing you did was to look at your watch.

You didn't even attempt to guess. In fact you have no idea what the time is, because you have something that tells you what the time is—so you don't have to bother. And that's exactly where Trevor is at this moment."

"Oh! I see. What are we looking for then?" Tariq asked. He now understood the importance of their task.

"Well, Tariq, the problem can be described in exactly one word, and that word is, '*clocks*'," Dave explained.

"Oh!"

Dave carried on, "Roughly speaking, anything that has hands on it, which point to numbers, can be considered a clock." Dave thought about what he'd said then added, "And anything with numbers on it, that does not have hands, can also be considered a clock."

"Okay. And that's it then?" Tariq asked. He wanted to make sure he was going to do the right thing.

"Yes," Dave replied. He went on to describe how they would, together, seek out all of the clocks in Trevor's house. "To cover the entire house as quickly as possible we'll need to split up," Dave said. "I'll take the upstairs and you can take the downstairs. When we find any kind of clock thing, it needs to be broken; made unfixable, totally smashed to pieces."

Tariq nodded. It was now clear to him why they should smash everything they came across.

"I'll pile mine up at the top of the stairs," Dave continued, "and you pile yours in this kitchen. Once we've finished we'll dispose of them."

"Okay. And to do this we'll split up?" Tariq asked. He didn't like the idea of splitting up and was getting worried at the prospect. Although Tariq liked to think he was as brave as Dave, he knew he wasn't.

"Yep. That okay?" Dave asked.

"Of course it is," Tariq answered as he smiled. "What do you think I am? Some kind of wuss?" Tariq finished; pretending he wasn't.

"No! Of course I don't. Are you sure about what you need to do?"

"Absolutely, Dave. I'll start at the front of the house and work my way to the back. Where do we meet?"

"When we're finished we'll meet at this see-through flap thing," Dave said.

"Right. Off we go then?" Tariq said.

"Yep. Off we go," Dave said.

"How long do we have?" asked Tariq.

"Well, according to the dog," Dave said, "he can keep them out of here for about an hour."

"Is that enough time?"

"It has to be. We've no choice. If we work fast enough then it should be," Dave said.

As fast as he could Dave made his way up the stairs of the Emits' home, to the upper floors. At the same time Tariq made his way to the lounge, which was at the front of their house.

Chapter 19.
Breaking Time

Tariq had never ever felt this nervous, so scared, and so worried in all his life before. *This should be Dave's job*, he thought. Not his. But Tariq knew in his heart that there was no way Dave would be able to tackle a job this size all on his own; especially in the time they had to complete it.

Tariq entered the parquet-floored lounge, its polished wooden squares made the floor quite slippy. He glanced back over his shoulder at Dave. Dave had started to make his way up the stairs.

Tariq saw his first clock; it was on the mantelpiece above the fireplace in the lounge. *How can I get to that?* he thought. He was only the height of a tortoise.

THUD, DONK, CLANK, DONK, PING, DONK, THUD.

The noise set Tariq shaking, what on earth was that? He poked his head out of the lounge and saw the pieces of a broken clock at the bottom of the staircase.

Phew, he thought, *that must've been Dave's first clock*.

Back to the task at hand. Tariq noticed a beige leather wheelie footstool in the middle of the lounge floor. He knew it would help him, so he pushed it towards the marble surrounded fireplace.

As he jumped onto the footstool it glided across the floor towards his target. But the footstall was not under any kind of control and started to rotate. Tariq reached for the clock in an attempt to capture it from the mantelpiece. He sent the clock spinning towards the floor.

Excellent, he thought. That was his first one. Feeling much better he looked around the rest of the room. No more in here; time to move on to the next room. Into the dining room he went.

"Oh my god!" Tariq exclaimed as he looked up at the huge pendulum clock. The clock was attached to the dining room wall; it was a good one and a half metres above the floor. *How on earth am I going to get that?* he asked himself.

THUD, DONK, CLANK, DONK, PING, DONK, THUD.

Tariq dived into his shell.

"Oi!" said Shell. "What are you playing at? You know I will leave you, don't you?"

"Shell! This just isn't the time or the place," Tariq answered.

"Why are we here? This isn't our hutch. Are you doing something you shouldn't?" Shell continued.

"Just don't, Shell. I've no time to explain," Tariq said.

"Just don't what?" Shell demanded.

"Shell! Please! I'll explain later, but not just now. Okay?"

"Do you really think you can put me off that easily?" Shell said.

"Shell—Please—I'm trying to do something important," Tariq said.

Shell started laughing. "Important? You? Are you kidding?"

"NO! I AM NOT," Tariq said firmly.

Shell was more than slightly shocked by Tariq's tone.

"You really are trying to do something important then?" Shell questioned.

"Yes."

"Really?" Shell asked once more, trying to make sure Tariq was telling the truth.

"YES!" Tariq said again, but with a little more force this time.

"Okay. Tell me later," Shell said.

"I will. Can I get on now?" Tariq said in a manner which meant he would not take an answer that said otherwise.

"I suppose so," Shell said in a huff.

Tariq reached into his satchel and pulled out a couple of heavy duty springs. *I think these may do the trick,* Tariq said to himself as he attached the springs to his feet. Once they were on he started to bounce. "Please forgive me, Shell," he said.

Tariq leapt up and down. When he'd reached the right speed he aimed himself at the wall clock. The next bounce launched him into the air. Just before he made contact he retreated into his shell.

CRUNCH!

He hit the clock full force.

TWANG, CRACK, SMASH.

The clock came away from the wall and fell to the floor.

"Ouch," said Shell.

"It didn't hurt that much, Shell. Stop whinging." Shell didn't say anything else.

Tariq was over the moon; what a success! The only problem he had now was how he was going to stop himself bouncing around the room forever.

After bouncing from the floor for the fifty millionth time he managed to reach one of his feet as he flew through the air. He dislodged a spring from his left foot.

Tremendous, he thought. But as soon as the thought had passed through his head he realised he was about to hit the floor with only one spring on one foot. He changed his mind and thought, *OH NO!*

Tariq hit the floor hard on his only remaining spring. Then he bounced from the floor at a strange angle, and zoomed through the air. As he did he cartwheeled, in the same fashion a carrot would if it'd been used as an orange coloured Frisbee.

Tariq knew it was going to get a bit bumpy. He retreated back into his shell once again, and held on for his life.

As the tortoise-shaped Frisbee twisted through the air the spring, attached to Tariq's foot, caught glimpses of the rising sun on its silvered surface through the dining room's windows.

Propelled by the spring Tariq bumped into odd bits of furniture in the room, a coffee table, another mantelpiece, some light fittings, and a weird umbrella stand.

On his back, eventually, Tariq's spin slowed. He popped his head and arms out of Shell and held them in the same position anyone would if they were performing a "snow angel". Bit by bit he stopped spinning. Once stationary he removed the final spring from his foot.

Hmmm, he thought, *probably not the best decision I've ever made*.

Tariq moved the remnants of the clocks into the kitchen. Since he'd disabled the remaining clocks in the lounge and the dining room, all he had left to tackle were those in the kitchen. Tariq stood, dusted himself off, and made his way to the kitchen and his final tasks.

On the oven, and microwave, there were the usual digital clocks. He disposed of those by loading some broken bits and pieces from the other room onto one of the springs, pulling it back, and then simply letting it go. The bits of broken furniture and clock, from the lounge, hit the oven's display; the force smashed the clocks.

Although broken, the remains of the oven's digital display sparked as electricity short circuited within it—broken wires touching other wires that should never have been in contact.

Tariq checked the kitchen cupboards, one by one, and each of them were empty.

But when he opened the last one there was a most peculiar looking grey box-like clock. It had a red hand, it had a black hand, and it had grey tubes attached to it.

Tariq knew this had to be the last clock he would have to deal with. What it looked like didn't matter. It was the end of the task to help Trevor and his family.

Tariq pulled at it. He heaved it, and he pushed it. The clock would not yield. It was not going to give way. He made a final attempt. He wedged a spatula, one he'd found in one of the kitchen cupboards, between the back of the grey clock and the wall. With a great effort he managed to unfix it from the wall. The clock with the red and black hands came away, and Tariq was relieved; he'd done his job, completed the task as Dave had asked.

But then a loud and angry hissing sound started. Tariq moved back from the cupboard as fast as he could, then looked in. All he could see, in the dim light of the cupboard, was some kind of greyish ribbed snake, its mouth open in a big 'O' shape, and it hissed at him.

"Snakes!" Tariq screamed. He didn't like snakes one bit. He had to find Dave. Dave would know what to do.

Tariq scarpered from the kitchen faster than a tortoise on springs. He stopped at the bottom of the staircase to the upper level of the Emits' home, and looked up at the incredibly steep slope.

Tariq's heart sunk. *Oh my God*, he thought, as he paused to decide what to do.

He heard the hissing once again from the kitchen, then smelt an awful rotten egg smell. His decision was made. He legged it up the stairs as fast as his little legs could take him. Any onlookers would have thought Tariq had moved up the stairs faster than any tortoise ought to be able to.

It was only when Tariq had reached the top he wondered how he'd managed it. But that was not important.

"Dave! Dave, there's something really wrong. The clock had a snake in it. A snake! Can you believe that?" Tariq said.

Dave poked his head out of the room he was in. "What are you going on about, Tariq?" he said. "Snakes in clocks? You've got to be mistaken."

"No! No," Tariq replied.

Tariq was looking worse than Dave had ever seen him before, paler than pale. "Don't worry, Tariq. Only one more clock up here on the mantelpiece to sort out. Once we've dealt with that, I'll go down and have a look for you," Dave said. He hoped his comments would calm his friend.

"Thanks, Dave," Tariq said. He was relieved that Dave seemed to have everything under control.

They crossed the room to the fireplace; Tariq could now help Dave reach the solitary final clock, which was perched on the mantelpiece.

Together the two friend pulled the clock to the floor; it broke into pieces.

"Tremendous," Tariq said. He'd no idea what would happen next.

Chapter 20.
Gas

The gun-metal grey gas meter with its red and black hands was off the wall. Gas hissed and spilled from the broken pipe at an incredible rate. The pipe flicked back and forth in the air as the gas pumped from it. The pipe seemed to have a life of its own.

Bit by bit the kitchen filled with gas. All the while the oven's smashed display flashed and crackled with electrical sparks, sparks that jumped between the bare and exposed wires of the oven's display.

Inch by inch the gas fumes filled the kitchen from the floor up. With each belch of fumes from the pipe the invisible, but rotten-egg smelly gas drifted nearer and nearer to the oven's broken display.

Then the gas and display met.

In an instant, with one huge BOOM, the Emits' home suddenly and loudly rearranged itself into a badly stacked pile of bricks and rubble, as the gas from the broken pipe was ignited. The flame flashed through the cloud of gas and exploded.

Bricks, and glass, and doors, and a dog bowl, were thrown high into the air, much to the surprise of some starlings, who had to perform some very clever aerobatics to avoid being hit.

A large brick stopped moving towards the sky and started a crazy plunge back to the ground. It crashed through the grill which covered the drain next to the Emits' house; the Time Goblin's home, where it had hidden for many years. The place the goblin had found when It had discovered Trevor's problem, the one of not knowing his own history.

The brick mashed the Time Goblin's head as it landed and forced bits of drain cover into its skull. The goblin's life force was bashed out of it, and the Time Goblin turned back into the mud and slime from which it had been made.

All that remained of the Emit family's house, was the chimney stack. Where the first floor had been, only the hearth of the fireplace remained; still attached to the chimney stack. It was on this hearth that Dave and Tariq stood. They looked at each other, quite surprised.

"Oh!" Tariq said to Dave.

"Oh!" Dave agreed.

"Well, we got rid of the clocks then," Tariq said trying to put what had happened in the best possible light.

"Yeah," replied Dave, still totally gob-smacked.

"Quite a good view really, once you get rid of the walls," Tariq said.

"I suppose it is," Dave said.

"Do you think they'll notice?" Tariq said as he thought about the soon to return Emits and their dog.

"Well, I suppose we could suggest it was some kind of make-over by *DIY SOS* or something."

"What?" Tariq asked.

Dave and Tariq were now exposed to the elements

"No. I didn't buy that either." Dave was gradually coming out of his shock.

Without the walls of the house Dave and Tariq were now exposed to the elements. The wind gusted around them. Dave was having trouble remaining on the hearth.

"Oh great," Dave exclaimed as he noticed his trolley was now exposed and the hedge seemed to have got up and left at some stage. "I never got to wear my flexi-crete suit!"

"Seventh! Is that you?" a voice boomed. It seemed to come from everywhere.

Dave looked from left to right. Who was calling him by his old name? It certainly wasn't Tariq. Somehow he recognised the voice, but couldn't quite place it.

"It is you!" Jonesy said, as he flew down to the chimney stack. "I was wondering where you'd got to."

"Jonesy! What are you doing here?" Dave asked.

"Some problem with the holiday lake not being finished. Couldn't really understand what they were trying to say. Decided to come back. Who's this?" Jonesy said looking at Tariq.

"That's Tariq. He's been helping me to do some amazing things," Dave said.

"It's good to hear you haven't been wasting your time since you left us. I like the chimney stack. Reminds me of a pile of bricks I was once acquainted with," Jonesy said.

Dave surveyed the remains of the Emits' house. From their vantage point, one floor up and no walls, Dave could see the park where the Emits had taken the dog for a walk, which was not strictly true as it was where the dog had gone to take the Emits for a walk.

Worryingly Dave saw that the dog and the Emits had almost finished In the park. Well, for certain, the dog had, as it had started to make its way to the park's exit.

"Jonesy, I don't suppose you could give me and Tariq a lift could you?"

I don't suppose you could give me a lift?

"Anything for you, young sir," Jonesy said.

"We need to go over there," Dave said, and pointed to Tariq's hutch which was at the back of a house a couple of blocks up the road.

"Okay, grab hold."

"Thanks, Jonesy."

With that Tariq and Dave grabbed hold of a claw each, and Jonesy swooshed his huge wings. Up and away they went off towards Tariq's home.

Chapter 21.
Dogs Don't Like Rubble

The dog pulled at his lead as it dangled from Trevor's hand. He was sure an hour had passed, and it sounded as if a storm was on the way. The dog was certain it had heard some thunder.

Trevor picked up a twig and threw it towards the centre of the park, totally misunderstanding the dog's intention. The dog let the lead drop from its mouth as it gazed at the twig. It sat down. The twig twisted and spun through the air before it landed next to an old oak tree a few tens of meters away. The dog looked up at Trevor. Trevor raised his eyebrows and mouthed, *Go on then, dog*. The dog stood up and started to trot towards the park's exit, tail in the air. He hoped the crazy feather in the yellow running suit, and the tortoise, had fixed whichever problem they thought his tick had been suffering from.

Trevor looked at the twig and then at the dog as it retreated. Trevor gave in. "Dog! Come here, boy. I've got to put your lead on."

"Oh. Leave him, Trevor. He's quite happy," Daphne cajoled.

"He's got to go on a lead, Daphne. Can't be too careful."

The dog scampered up the road ahead of Trevor and Daphne. Its owners struggled to keep up. The dog turned the corner, onto its road, and stopped. As it stared at the dog bowl in the middle of the pavement, the dog frowned. It shook its head. But just to make sure it sniffed the bowl, then leapt back as if someone had just tasered its nose. The dog sat on its haunches and scratched an ear with one of its rear legs. The dog was thoroughly confused. *How on earth can my bowl be here; at the top of the road?* it wondered. The dog stood up. It couldn't wait for its owners, who were taking their time. It had to find out more.

The dog started up the street with its nose pressed to the ground as it attempted to sniff out the reason for the mysterious appearance of its bowl on the street, and why it was not in the kitchen where it should be. Its little black nose twitched as the dog inhaled the aromas from the path it followed.

For the second time the dog stopped abruptly. This time it wished it had hands like its human owners; it had followed a scent and had not noticed the partial remnants of a wall in its path. It dearly wished it could rub its nose to take the pain away. Instead it decided to bark. "Woof," the dog said. Then shrugged its shoulders. Barking hadn't helped at all. Its nose still hurt.

This is very strange, the dog thought. *First my bowl, then part of a wall!* Like all dogs it couldn't see very well. It leant into the partial wall to get a better look. Then leapt back like before. *The garden wall!* it thought, utterly astounded. *My garden wall!* it thought further. The dog was now very worried, but it decided to continue on up the road to its home.

As it was just about to turn into its masters' driveway it tripped over a brick and landed flat on its stomach. The dog picked itself up, glared at the brick, which shouldn't have been there, then carried on up the driveway more determined than ever.

All of a sudden its back legs gave way as the impossible registered in its head. The dog collapsed onto its haunches and stared. It didn't need good eyesight to see this.

"OH MY DOG!" the dog said. "How stupid was I to think that that crazy feather and that weird and rude tortoise could stop my nervous tick? They've destroyed my masters' home. If I ever see them again..."

Both Trevor and Daphne frowned at the different things they saw strewn across the pavement, and road, and on the grass verge, as they made their way back home from the park.

Daphne had even picked up their dog's bowl on the way. She hadn't questioned the reason for it being in the middle of the street simply because she'd been with Trevor for so long, she'd got used to the many weird things that happened around him.

"Oh! Trevor!" said Daphne as she reached the entrance to what used to be their front garden and house. "Aren't we lucky?"

Trevor's thought was completely different. His chin nearly hit the floor. Twice! Once because his lovely home was now just a pile of bricks and rubble, and the second time because, for some inexplicable reason, Daphne thought they were lucky. The shock must have got to her, he thought.

"Why are we lucky? Our house has gone! Our garden has gone! It's all gone! It's all been—totally destroyed," Trevor said as he tried to grasp the enormity of the situation.

"We're lucky because of the dog," replied Daphne.

"Because of the dog?" Trevor asked, completely gob-smacked by his wife's comment. "Because the dog is alive?" he said as he tried to understand what his wife was proposing.

"No. Because the dog must have known something really bad was going to happen. It got us out of the house didn't it?" his wife answered.

"I suppose you're right, Daphne," said Trevor. But he didn't feel lucky. He had no job and no way of ever buying another house, and Daphne didn't know he hadn't been keeping up the insurance payments on their home, for the simple reason he was not earning any money. He was sure she would leave him now, once she'd found out this little titbit of information.

Trevor had had enough. What a miserable life he'd had, and to bring Daphne into it as well.

If only I could click my fingers just like this and turn back time, Trevor thought as he clicked his fingers and hoped beyond hope everything would somehow be all right, not knowing he was a Time Guardian without a Time Goblin to do battle with any longer.

Chapter 22.
No Problem

Morning was breaking. It was 7:14 a.m. Trevor opened his eyes; he had been roused by the *click, click, click,* of a bicycle freewheeling. It was the postman.

The postman rested his bike against the front wall of the house, against the hedge. The postman walked along the garden's cracked and chipped concrete path to the front door.

He plunged his hand into his postbag and pulled out a single letter, then pushed it into the letter box. It was one of those letter boxes which attached to the front of the house. One that required the owners of the house to leave their front door and collect their post from the box on the wall.

The postman about faced, walked back down the cracked pathway and got back on his bike then headed for the next address that required a delivery.

* * *

Trevor woke up. His radio alarm clock blasted out the news from the local radio station. He reached over and turned the volume down.

He couldn't ever recall feeling so refreshed from a night's sleep before. He threw back the duvet and got up. Trevor pulled on his dressing gown and went downstairs and walked along the hall into the kitchen to put the kettle on for a cup of coffee. The kettle boiled and he poured himself a large black coffee; just out of habit. He took a sip then made his way to the front of the house, cup in hand, and opened the front door. He stepped down the front door step and opened the post box. Inside there was a solitary letter. Trevor pulled it out. Before going back into the house he looked around; the air had the touch of winter about it, but the sky was the bluest of blues he'd ever seen, and the sun's rays had just started to break over the horizon. He took a deep breath. He couldn't put his finger on it but for some reason things felt a little different, a little better. Trevor walked back into his house and closed the front door behind him.

The dog trotted from the back garden, along the path next to the house and wandered round to the front; almost as if to see whether Trevor had managed to get the letter the postman had delivered.

The tick peeked out from the hair on the dog's head and started to feel relaxed. "Relaxed!" it said to itself. This was certainly a new sensation. There was no sign of the horrid little green man with its stupid and horrible purple pointy hat, nor its horrid nasty wooden frame. Perhaps the tick didn't need to find a way to leave after all.

After the tick had double checked, once more, that the coast was clear, and there *really* was no sign of the horrid little green man, the tick disappeared and then reappeared with its deck chair and hamper.

Within a few moments it had found a place on the dog's head where the hair was not as thick as it was in other places. The tick opened up its deck chair and placed its picnic basket next to the chair. The tick took a book from the inside pocket of its jacket and placed it next to the hamper. Then it opened the basket and took out a pot of steaming tea. The tick proceeded to pour itself a cup and using the sugar tongs it dropped five cubes of sugar into its tea, then began to stir the tea with vigour. Once its tea was ready, properly stirred, it closed the hamper's lid and placed its tea pot and cup on the basket's top. The tick then sat back in its deck chair and put on its reading glasses. The tick was now ready to enjoy the rest of its day, and ready to read its favourite book by H.G. Wells; *The Time Machine*.

Inside the house, in his kitchen, Trevor opened the letter, read it, and looked at where he thought he had a watch.

"Strange, I thought I had one," Trevor muttered to himself and then thought, *Somehow this all seems vaguely familiar.*

Trevor walked through his house looking for a clock. He couldn't find one anywhere, and actually he felt he really didn't need one.

"Trevor, what does the letter say?" Daphne called down from upstairs. She knew it was Trevor's habit to check the letter box before anything else he decided to do during the day.

"It says I need to turn up at the new job by 10:15 a.m."

"What's the time now?" she asked.

"7:33 a.m. and 24 seconds" Trevor said, automatically. And then he frowned whilst he covered his now gaping mouth with his hand. He had a little think. *Where did that come from?* he wondered.

"At least that gives you plenty of time to get ready then," said Daphne.

"Yes, it does," Trevor replied with absolute certainty. "Do you fancy taking the dog for a walk first?" Trevor asked.

From somewhere inside he felt a new confidence grow, and knew that from this day forward he would never fall foul of time ever again.

About the Author

 Simon needed to do something very special for his daughters, for their Christmas present. Although he'd worked in I.T. for over 15 years, at the time, and knew about project planning, what he decided to take on was completely out of his comfort zone and capability, and this fact was to be adequately demonstrated on more than one occasion.

In his naivety, he decided to write a story about a super hero whose only superpower was the fact that he had impossibly deep pockets. Once done Simon would wrap the book up, in amazing Christmas paper, and hand a copy to each of his daughters: this was in February 2003, the goal being to hand the "amazing" present to them around 25th December 2003—and that is where the project totally fell apart.

It took Simon a couple of months to finish writing the story, but as he wanted it to be the best for Molly and Tilly; as any father would, he sent the manuscript to a professional literary agency to garner their opinion. The result; "an original story", and to paraphrase now, "but the writing is crap". Simon was shocked. He'd paid for the analysis and they'd told him it was crap – that's a sure sign of professionalism; the agency had done what they'd been paid for – no sucking up.

Of course, they were right; Simon hadn't been trained, so he embarked on multiple writing courses, including script writing courses, then rewrote the story. By the time he'd completed this endeavour he'd missed Christmas 2003 by 18 months! But he continued simply because it is his philosophy that if you don't do anything to achieve your goal, you'll never achieve your goal.

Now he has an agent. It has been a long and informative journey for Simon; somewhat echoing Brave Dave's journey of learning, but he's pleased to acknowledge the journey hasn't finished yet. With three more novels in the series complete, and two others in the wings, he's certain you'll have enjoyed this first story, as it describes the beginnings of Brave Dave's education in the world of women, men, children and beasts.

<u>More in the Brave Dave series;</u>

A Hero in the Making

The Caribbean Conspiracy

A Space Oddity

www.BraveDave.co.uk

www.srwoodward.co.uk

Twitter: @srwoodwardUK

Facebook:

https://www.facebook.com/srwoodwarduk